MW01199905

*Dinner with a Highland Ghost*

*A Paranormal Romance*

*J.R. Barrett*

*Dinner with a Highland Ghost*

*Because I promised myself one day my hero would wear a kilt.* —*J.R. Barrett*

★ ★ ★

*Emma said to me, "It wasn't true love because it was easy. True love is hard."*

*Dinner with A Highland Ghost*

*Emma wriggled her hand through her stuffed backpack, searching for the slick copy of Food and Wine Magazine.*

*Ah, there it is.*

*With a satisfied smile she tossed the magazine onto her fully reclining seat in her private space age pod, or whatever her private seat was called.*

*First class. Sweet.*

*A flight attendant stopped beside her.*

*"Welcome aboard, Miss Steen. Let me help you with that bag." Emma's backpack vanished into a nearby closet. "Would you care for a glass of champagne before takeoff?"*

*"Oh yeah," said Emma, grinning from ear to ear. "I'd love one."*

*The round-trip first-class ticket was a birthday gift from her family. In fact, her family had presented her with the entire trip last April. It was her reward for surviving five years with Tom and then walking away. She was free—poor as a church mouse but free as a bird.*

*The attendant handed her a crystal champagne flute and poured.*

*"Thanks."*

*Emma glanced around the cabin. She wanted to make certain the other passengers were ignoring her. She lifted the glass in a silent toast—To Tom, may you live long and prosper, far away from me.*

*She plopped down into her seat and curled onto her side, studying her little pod with wonder. The seat transformed into a bed with the press of a button. It came equipped with a movable glass privacy screen, her own television, headphones, an eye mask, a zipper bag of toiletries. She couldn't help but waggle her eyebrows.*

*So, this is how the other half lives.*

*Emma sipped the sparkling wine. It was nicely chilled and tasty. She resisted the urge to smack her lips in satisfaction. She assumed one did not smack one's lips in first class.*

*It was late September and Emma was on her way to Scotland. She'd reserved a self-catering cottage located on the quiet shore of Loch Ness, southwest of Inverness. She'd reserved the cottage for four beautiful weeks of autumn weather, real autumn weather.*

*Wow.*

*Emma was so sick of heat, more like exhausted. Phoenix was still suffering through one of its typical long hot summers and she relished the notion of hiking through fog, rain, and a brisk wind. She wouldn't even mind a little snow. Why, it had been so scorching hot she wouldn't complain about a full-blown blizzard.*

*Whoever said dry heat was better than humidity was either crazy or full of baloney. Most days Emma felt like she lived in the middle of a convection oven. A month ago, it had been so hot, one-hundred and twenty-six-degrees Fahrenheit at noon, that she'd carried two eggs outside and tried to fry them on the black asphalt in front of her* mailbox. Just to be contrary, maybe prove a point to the weather gods. The eggs hadn't fried but they'd dehydrated within the hour. The mailman had rung her doorbell, and with a big grin, asked if he could have a side of wheat toast.

"We didn't even have much of a monsoon season this year."

The woman on the other side of the glass partition chimed in. "Amen to that, honey. You ain't kiddin'."

Emma lifted her glass high in agreement.

This year Phoenix had somehow skipped the glorious monsoon month; the month when the air grew thick and heavy and unnaturally still, and the sky boiled with glorious greenish black clouds.

Emma waited, her heart pounding with excitement, for those days. She would stand out on her deck and listen to the wind howl down the road, thick with desert dust and the occasional lightweight patio umbrella. Then she'd retreat inside to watch the lightning and cringe at the resulting crash of thunder while the rain poured down in sheets.

A good monsoon wasn't just a storm; it was a Noah's ark type deluge. The streets would flood. Outdoor furniture might end up in the pool or fly over the wall into the neighbor's yard. If the residents of Phoenix were especially lucky, someone would spot a funnel cloud.

Emma shivered at the image. *A good monsoon is way better than a night with my ex-husband. A good monsoon makes me feel alive.*

When the rains at last ceased for the day, Emma could always find a few interesting creepy-crawlies in her yard, creatures that had been washed out of the ground or blown in from the desert. She wasn't fond of black widow spiders, but scorpions, snakes and tarantulas didn't scare her, unless they were in her bedroom.

Or shared her bed.

Snakes were predictable most of the time, and Emma simply gave them a wide berth. Tarantulas weren't deadly poisonous and they generally wanted to get as far away from you as you wanted to get from them. Even black widows were shy, for the most part, although their bite was nasty. But scorpions were aggressive.

A scorpion had squeezed out from beneath a cabinet one morning after a heavy rain and scuttled straight at Emma from clear across her kitchen. She happened to have a sauté pan in her hand at the time and she'd slammed it down on the scorpion just before it reached her bare foot.

"Tom reminds me of a scorpion." Emma remembered her invisible seatmate on the other side of the partition and she was careful to keep her voice down.

Her ex-husband, Tom, lashed out mindlessly at anything he considered a potential threat. He was almost always apologetic afterwards, but it was too little too late. The damage had already been done.

Emma sipped her champagne, considering her ex-husband. Her divorce had been finalized in April. Five months ago. They'd separated seven months before that and she'd moved back into her house in Phoenix. He'd stayed in Jerome to run the restaurant. The restaurant she'd bought and paid for; built from nothing, the restaurant into which she'd poured her heart and soul. She'd only seen Tom once since the meeting in her lawyer's office. He'd come to visit friends in Phoenix and he'd taken the opportunity to return some of her CDs and a few of the cookbooks she'd forgotten in her haste to get the hell away from him. She'd left them on a shelf in their kitchen.

Well, it was Tom's kitchen now.

No hard feelings on her part. Honestly. Just five wasted years, two shattering miscarriages, and a boat load of money down the drain. He'd lost all her money. Every single cent.

Now Emma had to start from scratch. She felt a lot like she had when she'd first graduated from culinary school—scared to death. She didn't know whether to begin all over again, see if she could get financial backing for another restaurant, find a job as a sous chef, resume catering full time, or continue to work as a pastry chef for an hourly wage.

After the nightmare of the restaurant divorce war, it was a relief not to be saddled with so much responsibility, but still, she was currently overworked and underpaid, and the benefits weren't all that great.

Emma hoped this vacation would help her clear her mind, allow her to reach some decisions. She felt as if she'd put her life on hold for an entire year while she and Tom worked out their financial issues. She'd given up her ownership of the restaurant without protest, just to get out from under the pressures of working with him every day, *but that meant giving up the money, too. Tom didn't yet have the resources to buy her out. He'd agreed to give her half the money within three years, the remainder within six. Emma prayed he'd find a way to live up to his end of the bargain or she'd be out her entire life savings and then some. At least the home in Jerome was a rental and they'd transferred the lease into his name, so she didn't have to worry about selling another piece of her heart.*

*Emma gave herself an imaginary pat on the back. She'd been smart to keep her house in Phoenix as an investment even after she and Tom had married. He'd argued against it, said they could use the money for the restaurant. But Emma had resisted.*

*I probably knew I'd end up back in Phoenix one day, alone.*

*She'd always rented the house to tenants willing to sign a month to month lease. That had made it easier when she'd needed to move back home.*

*The attendant strolled up the aisle, stopping at Emma's seat. "Would you care for a refill?"*

*Emma hesitated for just a moment. She didn't usually drink in the middle of the day. For that matter, she didn't drink much at all.*

*Why not enjoy a refill? I'm not driving anywhere. I don't have to be in the bakery at four a.m. to fold the croissant dough. There are no sticky buns to put in the oven. No cakes to decorate and package for delivery. No tart shells to fill with lemon curd. No pate a choux to stir and steam-bake and fill with pastry cream and dip in chocolate ganache.*

She had none of her specialty cookies and cupcakes to bake and get into the cases. Someone else would have to do the best he or she could for an entire month. Emma held out her glass for a refill.

It was a nice crisp sparkling wine. Why not, indeed?

Emma held the crystal flute and settled deep into her comfy seat.

How luxurious!

She opened the copy of Food and Wine. She thumbed through the pages, eyeing the photos and skimming some of the recipes. A few of the more creative recipes piqued her interest. Emma was surprised to find she still had some interest in food. She hadn't cooked a real meal for herself in a long time.

It's no fun to eat alone. A good meal is meant to be shared with the people you love.

How true, and that's why I'm off to Scotland. If I'm going to be alone it might as well be some place magical.

Scotland promised to be an adventure and maybe, just maybe, the trip would change her luck. If nothing else, it would be a change in scenery.

As the jet taxied down the runway, picking up speed, Emma felt a familiar thrill run up her spine. It was the same thrill she experienced every time she flew. That initial arousal as their speed increased, the speed that forced her back into her seat, followed by the instant of disbelief as the heavy plane lifted off the runway, delicate as a butterfly.

As soon as the rear wheels left the ground, Emma closed her eyes and counted to *three hundred. Then, for good measure, she did it again. It was a superstition, like crossing her fingers or knocking on wood. She hoped if nothing happened during the first ten minutes after takeoff, nothing would.*

*At least nothing bad.*

*It was a control thing. Emma had issues with control. She was working on them, but it had eaten away at her marriage to Tom. He had his own major issues with control so the two of them butted heads constantly.*

*It's ironic, Emma thought as she thumbed through the magazine. The very thing that brought the two of us together drove us apart… a dream. The dream of owning a restaurant.*

*Perhaps she and Tom would have been better off remaining business associates instead of bedmates.*

*She rolled that thought around for a few moments as she'd done many times over the past few years. She came to the same conclusion she always did. No. That wouldn't have worked either. They were too much alike—stubborn, hard-headed and willful. Each determined to have things his and her own way. At least their parting had been somewhat more amiable than their marriage and working arrangement. The two of them would never be friends, but perhaps one day they could be colleagues again.*

*Nah. Dream on, girl.*

*When the plane leveled off, the ever-alert flight attendant strolled through the cabin once more. She handed Emma an embossed menu.*

*Emma glanced at the offerings. "Thank you. This is very impressive."*

*Lobster bisque? Chesapeake Bay crab cakes? Arugula salad with sun dried tomatoes, toasted pine nuts and capers? Skirt steak with wild rice or rack of lamb with fresh peas or halibut with a wild mushroom risotto? A German Riesling and a Napa Valley Cabernet Sauvignon?*

*She wondered how the passengers in coach were faring with their ubiquitous little bags of peanuts and plastic cups of ginger ale.*

*Life was so unfair sometimes.*

*Ah, there but for the pity of my family, go I.*

*Emma bit back a self-effacing laugh and chose the lobster bisque, the salad, the halibut and the Riesling.*

*No sad thoughts, she reminded herself. You promised on this trip. Put away your sadness. You have a chance to make a clean break of things and time to gain some perspective. No more blaming Tom. No more blaming the marriage. No more blaming yourself.*

*Yet she wondered once again, maybe for the millionth time, if she was to blame for losing her babies.*

*If I hadn't worked eighteen hours a day. If I'd gotten more sleep and remembered to eat regular meals. If Tom and I hadn't lost our tempers and spent more time yelling at each other than we did holding each other.*

*Shut up about the babies.*

*Losing the babies had just about shattered her heart. She started to put a hand on her chest. It was automatic, this need to rub away the ever-present ache. Emma forced herself to stop, to let her hand drop down onto the armrest.*

*It was better if she didn't go down that long, tortuous road.*

*Emma had always known she'd wanted children, a lot of them actually. It was the husband part that had never quite fit. Now she knew why. Maybe marriage wasn't in the cards for her.*

*More accurately, maybe marriage wasn't in the tea leaves.*

*Wasn't that what her great-grandmother had prophesied years ago? She'd looked in Emma's tea cup, swirled the leaves, and then stared at her for a moment before declaring Emma would never fall in love with any man alive.*

*Everyone in the room had laughed, including sixteen-year-old Emma. But later, when her relatives had headed off to watch some random Thanksgiving football game and it was just the two of them, Emma had asked her great-grandmother what the tea leaves meant. The elderly woman had merely repeated her words, "You will never be satisfied with any man alive."*

*"Well, what am I supposed to do? Fall in love with a ghost?"*

*Shooting Emma a wrinkled puckish grin, her great-grandmother answered, "I may know how to read the tea leaves, but I don't always know what they mean."*

*That prediction had haunted Emma ever since. Maybe it was the reason she'd been so quick to marry Tom, to prove the stinking tea leaves wrong.*

The attendant interrupted Emma's thoughts, handing her a hot towel for her hands and face. She helped her unfold her hidden tray table, then covered it with a fine linen cloth.

Emma anticipated the first course, the lobster bisque. It arrived in a china bowl, piping hot, along with a little basket of dinner rolls and real butter, a spotless white linen napkin and a full set of chilled silverware including a knife. Emma did a double-take. She thought the airlines had banned all knives.

*Wow.*

The young attendant poured her a full glass of the Riesling. "Just let me know when you want a refill." She smiled at her.

*Am I that obvious? Emma* made an effort to smile back. "Thank you."

Perhaps all first-class passengers were treated with such courtesy. Emma glanced around the cabin. She couldn't see very far because of the privacy screens. There was the invisible woman seated in the pod next to her, an older couple across the aisle and another couple across from them. The attendant was so, well, attentive, it felt as if the six of them had their own private attendant for the next five hours.

Emma knew the young woman was just doing her job, but she seemed sincere and she was darn good at it. The service was excellent. Each course was impressive, especially considering the fact that the food was airline food and the flight attendant had only a small galley at her disposal.

*Wonder what I could achieve in a small galley-sized kitchen?* She dismissed the *thought. I doubt I'll ever own another restaurant with or without a tiny kitchen.*

*Emma finished her meal and reclined her chair. She was contemplating a nap when the attendant brought by a dessert tray. Emma couldn't resist. Because she worked with so much sugar, she was careful about her intake, but she was a sucker for a good tasting. Emma helped herself to one of each of the tiny pastries.*

*The pistachio lime tart looked luscious, but the one bite she took was cloyingly sweet, so she set it aside. The cheesecake cup was nothing special, not worth the calories. She set that on the reject plate also.*

*With careful fingers Emma picked up the tiny, delicate profiterole. She nibbled the side, making sure to get some of the chocolate ganache icing. It was darn good—light, airy, fresh. She popped it into her mouth so the flavors and textures could mingle on her tongue all at once. Nice. Not as perfect as hers, but nice just the same.*

*The raspberry mousse gagged her. Too sweet. Reject.*

*Her favorites were the two itty-bitty bitter-sweet chocolate shortbread cookies with a salted caramel drizzle. Yum. Emma's taste buds quickly deconstructed the components and she was in the midst of mentally redesigning the cookie to make it even bigger and better when the attendant rolled up a freezer cart.*

*"Would you care for a hot fudge sundae?"*

*Emma couldn't hold back a snort. "You haven't stuffed enough food into me? You'll be using that cart to roll me off the plane in Newark. No, thank you."*

*"No, really." The flight attendant lifted an ice-cold ceramic bowl from her little*

*freezer.* "First class is only half-full, and I'm bored to tears. Let me make a sundae for you. The ice cream is great. It's organic. I've got chocolate, vanilla and strawberry. Hot fudge topping, caramel, strawberry, raspberry, whipped cream, nuts... C'mon, you won't be disappointed. Please?"

"How can I say no?" The woman's enthusiasm was contagious. "Okay, just a small scoop of vanilla and some hot fudge, that's it. No nuts, no whipped cream."

"How about a cherry?"

"Fine, you can top it with a cherry," said Emma.

"You know," said the young woman as she handed Emma the sundae, "I'll be serving you a cheeseburger with all the fixings in about three hours."

"You're kidding?" Emma giggled, nearly losing her hold on the cold bowl of ice cream. "What do you plan to do? Feed us for five straight hours? What about the people in coach?"

The woman winked at her. "Peanuts and pretzels," she said. "No, actually they have a menu. They can buy food if they wish."

"Yeah, that would usually be me. I'm a peanuts and pretzel kind of flyer." Emma grinned. "After this sundae, no more food. And in case you didn't hear that, let me repeat the words. No more food."

\* \* \*

*The flight to Newark was pleasantly uneventful. Emma dozed for an hour or so after her sundae then she watched a portion of an in-flight movie. She did manage to resist the tempting cheeseburger offered during the final leg of her journey.*

*After giving her flight attendant a cheery hug of gratitude for the pleasant service, Emma disembarked. Since her large backpack was checked through all the way to Edinburgh, Emma's only task in the Newark airport was to find the gate for her next flight. She scanned the board for the scheduled departures, found hers, and made her way to the International terminal only to be informed by an airline representative that her gate had been changed. It was back in the other terminal, right next to her arrival gate. She would have to go through security all over again.*

*"Well, at least I'm getting a little exercise after eating and sitting for five hours straight."*

*She passed a book store and doubled back to buy a newspaper and check out the rack of best sellers. The only thing she'd forgotten to pack was a book. She wanted something light for this trip, so she skimmed the romance titles. If her great-grandmother was correct and there was no man out there for her in this big wide world, she might as well spend a few hours with a fantasy lover.*

*Emma chose a book with a sedate-ish cover. It had nothing on it but a ruined castle and a kilted Highlander. She didn't want anything super sexy. Even though chances were no one would notice the book or care, she didn't feel like giving off a vibe that no man had touched her in that way for over two years.*

*She and Tom had slept apart since the night she'd caught him in the walk-in cooler with their very attractive, very female, sommelier.*

*Emma felt a twinge of anger.*

*Oh, for goodness' sake, Emma scolded herself, get over it. He did. He got over it real fast and moved on to the hostess.*

*But she couldn't deny she was lonely.*

*Emma was twenty-nine years old. She'd spent five years in a marriage she'd known was loveless after the first six months, hoping to save it anyway. She'd lost two babies while she'd busied herself helplessly hoping. To say her ego had taken a hit was an understatement. Emma wished she could kick her own ass for being so stupid.*

*For lack of a better word, she had never in her entire life felt so, well, so lacking as a woman. Tom had never made any attempt to hide the fact that he found her lacking. And she'd bought into his attitude and blamed herself for the failed marriage, for the babies.*

*Remember, this trip is not about Tom. This trip is about you. It's about finding yourself all over again, regaining your true self.*

*Emma shook her head, deliberately shaking off the bad memories. She made her purchases and headed toward the correct terminal. She had two hours to kill. She decided to spend it walking around the airport before she had to board another plane and sit for another six hours and eat two or three more gourmet meals.*

*\* \* \**

*John McGregor was adrift in a dream, or at least what passed for a dream in his present state. At first, he couldn't see much aside from the same mist he passed through every time he dreamed.*

*Gradually John's vision cleared but visualizing his surroundings didn't help him focus. The long, stark corridor through which he floated was not only unfamiliar, it made no sense to him. He had no context by which to judge it.*

*Normally when he fell into one of these dream states he would revisit the past, his past. He always assumed he was reliving memories, nothing more. But this? John had never seen anything quite like this place. The building in which he found himself lacked any natural color. It seemed to be primarily shades of white and gray. The floors were shiny, almost metallic in appearance, the ceilings very high, the windows covered with a thick tinted glass. Many large alcoves branched off both sides of the wide corridor where scores of people sat, scattered and separate, on bench-like seats. Most people strode purposefully through the corridor while others appeared to wander, aimless, as if they were in a kind of limbo. Most seemed to be waiting for something, but he knew not what.*

*The people he passed were dressed in what he'd come to think of as modern garb. John wondered, as he had for years, how on earth people could be comfortable wearing such restrictive clothing. But this was nothing more than a passing thought. What modern people did and didn't do meant little to him.*

*He floated among them, unnoticed and unseen, at least as far as he could ascertain.*

*No one had ever seen him when he dreamed these dreams or experienced these visions, he wasn't quite sure which they were, just as he wasn't quite sure where he vas.*

*There was a time, centuries ago, when he had returned to his home on Raasay and he'd seen his wife and son. He'd reached for them, desperate to take them both into his arms; to touch them, hold them. He'd wanted to explain his absence, but they hadn't been able to hear his words or feel his hands.*

*All too soon he'd been pulled away, sucked back to his mountains.*

*His wife, Tessa, had not even known yet that he had died. He believed she still clung to the hope that he would make his way home somehow, by some miracle, along with the other scarred refugees from Culloden.*

*She did not know he'd died alone in a rock hollow in the mountains above Loch Ness a month after the battle, a month after the incomparably brave, reckless, suicidal charge of the Highlanders on a boggy piece of land outside of Inverness.*

*The short, bloody battle at Drummossie Moor had taken the lives of his three brothers, his two uncles, and many of his cousins and his friends. Afterwards the Duke of Cumberland, the Butcher Cumberland, and his troops carried their blood lust to every corner of the Highlands, destroying an entire way of life, John's way of life.*

*John didn't know whether his wife and son had survived the slaughter and the season of starvation that followed. If they had managed to survive, he surmised they had been shipped off to the Colonies like so many others.*

*Because he couldn't bear to know the truth of the matter, he'd never tried to return to Raasay.*

*Ignorance might not be bliss, but it was better than the alternative.*

*Two hundred and seventy years had passed, but the death of the Highlands was still a dagger in his heart.*

*John remembered the battle like it was yesterday.*

*When the men of his family had met to discuss the rebellion, he had counseled patience. He'd only been married a year, he was still growing accustomed to life on Raasay with his wife's MacLeod clan. His wife had just delivered a son.*

*John was trained as a soldier, but he had no wish to die for the misguided dreams of a pretend king.*

*Yet when his brothers left to follow Bonnie Prince Charlie, he found it impossible to stay behind. John Charles McGregor was many things. One thing he was not was a coward.*

*As it happened, staying behind would have changed nothing. Because of his clan alone he would have been arrested and hanged and his wife and son left to starve if they hadn't been murdered outright.*

*He had come to realize that as the years passed. A McGregor male of fighting age would not have been left alive.*

*So much suffering. So many useless deaths.*

*For decades after his own demise, John had prowled the mountains like a beast, driven near to madness, first by the horrors he witnessed and then by the silence. For a long time, it was as if even the squirrels feared to leave their trees.*

*John was lonelier than he had ever imagined a man could be, even a dead man.*

*He'd wondered why he had been left behind. For years he'd railed at God and the Devil for abandoning him in purgatory. He'd tried to kill himself so many times he'd lost count, but a dead man couldn't kill himself, at least not for long.*

*No matter what he did, his soul would drift in the ether for a time and then return to his body. The only thing of which he was certain was that he had died. How he inhabited a body, how he could at times be a man and at other times a spirit was beyond his ken. He'd long ago given up trying to understand. It was just over the past hundred years or so that he'd begun to take an interest in his surroundings.*

*People had returned to the Highlands. At first it was a mere trickle, but in recent years the trickle had seemed like a flood. Of course, it was difficult to build homes in the mountains and the old villages and crofts remained ruins, but new homes had sprung up here and there. Once again children ran along the old village streets.*

*How he'd welcomed the laughter of children after centuries of nothing louder than birdsong.*

*A flutter of movement caught John's eye. A young woman strode through the corridor on long lean legs. Her hair tumbled down her back in a riot of mahogany curls, bouncing with each step. She carried some sort of pack, she'd slung it over one shoulder, and she held a publication in her hand.*

*Surprised to find his interest piqued, John allowed his body to drift down until he felt the hard floor tiles beneath his booted feet. It had been decades since he'd spared even a passing glance at a living, breathing woman. On a whim John turned and followed. After all, it was his dream and he had nothing better to do.*

\* \* \*

*The hair on the back of her neck prickled. It didn't just prickle, it stood straight up. Emma stopped in mid stride. She could swear someone was following her. She threw a quick glance over her shoulder. There was nobody there, at least nobody paying her any attention. But still... The footsteps, the sound of boots on the tile floor, had been very close, right behind her. It felt like someone had touched her. She could swear someone had run a hand over her hair.*

*A tingle crawled up Emma's spine.*

*Spooky.*

*Emma stood still for a long moment, then she turned in a full circle, but she saw nothing out of the ordinary. She stood all alone in the corridor.*

*Wow, okay, that was flat out weird. Either this airport is haunted, or my intuition is working overtime. Maybe I'm going the wrong way, or I've got some weird ESP warning me my flight has been changed.*

*Emma tried to shake off the odd feeling, but it was sticky, refused to leave.*

*It's a case of nerves. That's all it is.*

*Nevertheless, she decided to backtrack and head directly to her gate. She had a lot riding on this trip.*

*Wouldn't do to miss my flight.*

*Emma did an about face and headed toward her gate, but the uncomfortable sensation persisted. It would not go away. Well, the sound of the disembodied boots would not go away. She could swear she was being followed. As she hurried through the terminal Emma felt an overwhelming urge to sprint. She fought it, tried to slow her steps. The last thing she wanted to do was attract every security agent in the airport.*

*The sooner I board the plane the better.*

*She noticed a sign directing passengers to the First-Class Lounge.*

*Maybe I should hang out in there. It's secure. You have to have a first-class ticket to get in. If someone is following me what are the chances he's headed to Scotland and has a first-class ticket?*

*Emma dug her ticket and her ID out of her backpack and pushed open the door. She let it fall closed behind her, listening for the satisfying click. She glanced back to make certain, but the door remained closed. No one followed her.*

*"Hello, miss. Welcome to the British Airways lounge. May I please see your ticket and your photo ID?"*

*Emma handed them to the attendant with a sigh of relief. The disconcerting feeling had been nothing more than stress and a vivid imagination. The past five years had been that intense; it couldn't have been anything else. Yes, that was the only possible explanation. She was anxious about her past and worried about her future. Emma hoped this trip would help her make some sort of peace with both.*

\* \* \*

*John woke to another gray dawn. He was back where he'd been the night before, in his rudimentary shelter above the Loch. He'd lost her. The woman had disappeared behind a door and he'd been dragged away before he could follow.*

*He held his hand before his face. He opened his clenched fist and studied his lined palm, stared at his fingers. The silk of her hair lingered against his fingertips. He closed his eyes and inhaled, hoping to catch her fragrance. Like a whisper on the tendrils of mist that swirled about him, she was present. She was rich and red and feminine. She reminded him of the scent of hot house flowers and rare spices.*

*John sat up and squinted through the fog, praying he'd see her in the flesh, hoping she was more than a dream. But the memory threatened to vanish, just as she had vanished, and the mist left only a damp trail along his cheek.*

*The mountain plays tricks on a dead man.*

*"I din'nae find yer torments amusing, spirits," said John, using his voice to break her spell. He brushed the water from his face. "Nor do I enjoy a wet head."*

*He reached up, running a hand along the low roof of his rock shelter. "Every morning 'tis the same. Has'nae changed in…"*

*For an instant John couldn't remember how many years it had been, how long he'd haunted the mountains above the Loch. His heart sped up like a horse at a canter. The hoof beats in his chest thudded in his ears.*

*He'd been around so long he'd lost count of the days. Each day was the same day, one long hellish eternity of same days. They stretched before him, this never-ending joyless parade of mornings and evenings and moonrises.*

*John jumped to his feet. This would lead to no good. It would lead to another attempt at suicide.*

*And what would that accomplish?*

*Nothing.*

*He'd wake up right back in his cave. No better off than he was now. No closer to heaven. No farther from hell. Caught in this everlasting purgatory. And for what reason? What had he done to deserve such a punishment?*

*He had no answers because there were no answers to be found. John should know. He'd spent enough years searching.*

*John shoved his dirk into its sheath and sprinted from the glen. He needed distance from his thoughts. He ran down the slick, steep, winding trail to the shore of the loch as though the very devil pursued him. A dip in the icy waters of Loch Ness would do him good. Clear his head. Grant him space to breathe again.*

\* \* \*

*Emma waited until her crowded passenger car had emptied, then she hauled her big backpack off the luggage rack and tossed it out the door of the train. It landed on the platform with a satisfying thwack. Lugging it through the airport, onto a bus, and then through the train station in London had been a real pain.*

*She jumped down the two steps and looked around. Everyone else headed straight ahead so Emma hoisted both of her packs and followed. A rental car agency awaited her in the terminal. She was almost at the end of her journey. She faced one more challenge, a harrowing drive through Inverness then a short jaunt on the wrong side of a few country roads and she'd be able to say, the Highlands, at last. They would be hers for an entire month.*

*Emma took a deep breath, inhaling refreshing cool air along with exhaust from the cars passing outside on the busy street. She ignored the exhaust fumes, preferring to imagine how bracing the air would be once she was out of town. The mountains would be her private paradise. She could wade in her lake, er, loch. Visit her Fort William and Clava Cairns and Culloden and Castle Urquhardt.*

*She could even take her little car and head over to Skye for a few days of hiking and sightseeing. Maybe catch the car ferry at Ullapool and pay a visit to the Isles of Lewis and Harris and see the standing stones of Callanish. She could do whatever she wanted to do and there was nobody to tell her no. She could sleep late or get up early. She could eat, drink and be merry. For the first time in years Emma felt like a free woman.*

*Free. I'm footloose and fancy free.*

*Emma swallowed a giggle. She was acting like a giddy kid.*

*"Scotland. I'm in Scotland." Emma didn't know whether to pinch herself or kick up her heels. "I better quit acting like an idiot or they won't give me my car. It's bad enough I'm an American who's going to have to drive on the wrong side of the road. I don't want them to think I'm a drunk American who's going to have to drive on the wrong side of the road."*

* * *

The rental agent provided Emma with detailed driving directions. She followed his instructions to the letter until she left Inverness behind. Inverness wasn't all that big, but it seemed a whole lot bigger when you were jet-lagged, and you didn't know where you were going, and wherever it was you were going, you were going there on the wrong side of the road.

It was a relief to hit the single track along the wooded southeast shore of Loch Ness. There was only one way to go, straight ahead, and fortunately that side of the loch was lightly traveled with pullouts every couple hundred yards.

Emma made a point of repeating to herself, "Left. Pull to the left if you see another car."

She kept an eye on the odometer. The self-catering cottage was about twenty-four kilometers outside of town, almost directly across the loch from the picturesque ruins of Uruquhardt Castle.

Before she knew it, there she was.

Emma gave a long, low whistle as she idled in the narrow drive. The view was killer gorgeous. She turned off the ignition and sat there for a minute, awestruck, then she threw open the car door and climbed out, turning her head this way and that, wishing she could look in all directions at once.

Perfect. The cottage was perfect. Loch Ness was a short hike from her front door. The mountains rose, steep and silent, from the rear. She followed the footpath to the back of the house, inadvertently setting off a sudden birdie exodus from a row of feeders. Two squirrels scrambled up a tree. She watched them vanish into the leafy canopy.

"Ooh. Who knows? Maybe I'll be lucky enough to spot a pine marten."

Before she returned to her car, Emma stopped for a moment to study the dappled sunlight sprinkled like fairy dust over the dark blue waters of the loch. If she tossed her bags inside and threw the perishables she'd picked up at the local market into the fridge, she could get in a short hike before sunset.

"Oh, wow!" Emma hugged herself. "The air smells like a Christmas tree. I could bathe in this every single morning and never tire of it."

\* \* \*

Dripping hair tossed back over his equally wet shoulders, John Charles McGregor sat on a rock at the edge of the loch, a pile of carefully selected flat pebbles by his side. Few endeavors brought him peace. Sometimes pebbles did—tossing pebbles into the loch. It was a mindless activity. Mindlessness, when he could manage to achieve it, was something to be cherished.

John stood up on his bare feet and picked up a pebble. He sent it skimming over the surface of the loch, counting skips. "One, two, three, four, five…"

"Six. That's pretty good. I've never been able to skip a rock more than three times myself."

"What in the name of all that is holy…?" Pebbles in hand, a disbelieving John McGregor turned to stare at the woman.

"Sorry. I didn't mean to intrude. I just arrived, and I had to hike down to the lake, uh, I mean loch, and well, sorry. I didn't mean to disturb you." She backed off a pace.

"Who are ye talking to?"

She backed off another pace. "Um, you?"

John dropped the pebbles and strode toward her. He recognized her and once again his heart began to pound in his chest. It was the woman from his dream. He stopped within a foot of her. Yes. There was no mistake. His nostrils flared as he inhaled the same spice. "Who are ye? What sort of magic creature are ye? Are ye a witch?"

Her eyes darted to either side as if gauging whether or not she could outrun him. "Uh, I'm, uh, Emma. I'm an American." She waved a hand up the hill. "I'm renting that house, the one right up that path. Sorry. Really. I didn't mean to disturb you. I just wanted to get a closer look at the lake... loch... lake. It's my first visit to Scotland. Wait? Did you call me a witch?"

He stared at her. "Well, are ye a witch? Answer the question, woman. Are ye the reason I remain here?"

Her eyes opened wide and she shook her head. "A witch? The reason you're still here, at the lake, or loch?" The woman burst out laughing. "Where did that come from? Is this some quaint old Scottish custom? Welcome to Scotland. Are you a witch? Of course, I'm not a witch. Witches are make-believe. There's no such thing as a witch. I'm a baker. I bake cakes."

*"Ye do what?"*

*"I bake cakes, cookies, breads, pies, rolls. Listen..."* She edged away from him ever so slightly. *"I think I'd better be going now. I'm sorry I bothered you."*

*He reached out to her, wrapping his hand around her wrist. He held on, desperate for human contact. He knew he'd frightened her, but he couldn't help himself. She felt warm and alive beneath his fingers. And he wanted to cry. Instead he said, "Don'nae go, stay wi' me. Here..."* Still holding her arm, John leaned over to scoop up a fistful of rocks. *"Toss them. Aye. Toss them all into the loch."* He opened her hand and pressed the rocks into her palm. *"Stay. Talk wi' me. Let me hear yer voice again."*

*He let go of her arm and resumed his seat on the boulder. John attempted to form what he hoped was a reassuring smile, but he felt so out of practice he feared his face might crack.*

*The woman gamely stayed where she was, but she pointed to his ragged shirt where it lay draped over a tree branch. "You have goose bumps. You must be cold." She reached for the shirt and held it out to him. "Here."*

*He leaned over and took it from her hand. "I thank ye. I was..." John didn't know how to explain. He thought how ragged his clothes must look to her and he felt his cheeks burn. "I was swimming in the loch."*

*"You're kidding?" Her head turned, and she gazed out over the water. "Swimming with the monster?" She shook her head. "I couldn't do that. I could wade in a few feet, maybe, but that's as far as I'd go."*

John took the opportunity to study her profile by the light of the setting sun, marveling at her fine features and the delicate texture of her skin. He was awestruck by the fact that she could see him, hear him, speak with him.

After so many long centuries... It was a miracle.

"The water must be freezing." She tossed the pebbles into the water, leaned over to dip her hand in the resulting ripples. "Oh, it is freezing. No, I don't think I could swim in it, especially with the monster." She shot him a crooked grin.

John quickly pulled his shirt over his head. "The monster?" He stood up to tuck in the long tail, trying to make himself as presentable as possible. "Oh aye. Nessie, ye mean to say? I hae'nae seen her in many a year."

The woman's mouth dropped open and her eyes widened. "But you have seen her?"

He shrugged. "T'was long ago. She is no so bad as ye might think."

"Not so bad? But she's a sea monster."

John smiled. "She eats fish. She does'nae eat people."

The woman let go a peal of laughter. "You're teasing me, right? There is no Nessie."

"Oh aye, there is." He stood and brushed the dust from his rocky perch. "Would ye care to sit a spell? Perhaps she will make an appearance."

The woman studied the loch. He assumed she was looking for Nessie. At last she shook her head. "I don't, um, well... I just arrived, and I thought I'd hike along the shore before the sun sets. I don't know my way around, so I'd rather not be out after *dark, especially since I didn't get a good look at the lay of the land and these woods are pretty thick."*

*John's stomach twisted into a knot. After all these many years someone could see him, speak with him. He was loathe to let her out of his sight. There was a reason he'd dreamed of her. There had to be.*

*Perhaps her arrival heralded the end of his purgatory.*

*"I can walk with ye, show ye the way along the loch. I know the pathways like the back of my hand."*

*"Uh, no, that's all right. I wouldn't want to trouble you." Her eyes flitted here and there, lighting on the water, the rocks, the trees, anywhere but on his threadbare clothing. It was obvious he made her nervous.*

*And why not? He was a man out of time, a dead man at that. He should make her nervous.*

*"My name is John Charles McGregor." He stuck out a big hand.*

*She took it and he marveled once again at her living warmth. "Emma Rose Steen. I'm from Phoenix."*

*His unfamiliarity with the place name must have shown in his face.*

*"Phoenix, Arizona," she said. "It's in the desert southwest. You know, cacti, horses, cowboys and all that."*

*John shook his head. "I hae'nae heard of this place, but…"*

*Her laughter interrupted him. "But you've heard of America, right? You know, the Colonies."*

*"Ah, aye. I know of the Colonies."*

*She cocked her head at him. "You're pretty old-fashioned, aren't you? The way you say, the Colonies like we're still colonies?" Her eyebrows lifted. "We're not, you know. Colonies, I mean."*

*John didn't know how to answer. He'd paid little attention to the world. For that matter, he didn't even exist in her world.*

*"Well, it's nice meeting you, John Charles McGregor." She flashed him the barest hint of a smile. "But I'd better be going."*

*Before he could say another word, she turned and fled back up the path in the direction from which she'd come.*

*Damn.*

*John pulled on his worn leather boots as quick as he could; hopping from one foot to the other, trying to keep his balance and avoid falling over into the loch.*

*I will'nae lose her this time. Hell will freeze over first.*

\*  \*  \*

*Wow. That was weird. Emma hurried up the path toward her cottage, doing her best not to glance back over her shoulder. She worried some ghost might be chasing her. It felt like the airport in Newark all over again.*

*If I didn't know better, I'd say he was, oh, I don't know... a magic Scottish time traveler or something. He'd heard of the Colonies, but not the States? Either he's looney tunes or… Again, wow.*

*He was handsome though, awfully handsome, old-fashioned clothes notwithstanding. Although I have to admit he looks darn good wearing those clothes.*

*Maybe he just tosses on his old clothes when he swims in the lake, uh, loch.*

*Or maybe he's some Scottish independence guy who lives in the past, like our Civil War guys who reenact those Civil War battles.*

*Those old-fashioned clothes are sort of charming. Charming and sexy at the same time. Who wears a kilt these days, I mean outside of a ceremony?*

*Despite her concern about the man's mental health, the image of his wet bare chest, tight abs, and narrow hips seemed to be stuck in her mind like one of her warm caramel sticky buns. It preceded her along the trail, this floating vision of his masculine attributes.*

*He is cut, that's for sure. Whew. She fanned her face as she hiked up the hill. I haven't seen a man that cut since, well, since ever.*

*Crazy as a loon but pretty as a Scottish picture. Yummy Highlander sticky buns. Kinda makes me hungry.*

*Emma realized she hadn't eaten in hours. Hours and hours.*

*Gosh, when was the last time I ate? Breakfast on the plane? That was like, yesterday.*

*She had to stop and think. No, not yesterday, but it had been a long time since she'd eaten anything or slept for more than an hour or two. Even a cup of hot coffee would be welcome right about now.*

*Emma shivered. The sun had set and the cool breeze from the loch raised chill bumps on her bare arms. She'd been in such a hurry to get down to the shore it hadn't occurred to her to grab a jacket. Why should it? She was accustomed to the oven that was Phoenix.*

*How could he not know about Phoenix? He must be very out of touch up here. Probably doesn't even have internet.*

*Well, neither do I. Emma snorted. That's why I'm here. No internet. No television. No cell phone service. Just hiking and cooking and sleeping and sightseeing.*

*And maybe a fling with a hot wet long-haired bare-chested Scottish eccentric?*

*Emma stopped short. Where did that come from?*

*Chronic sex-deprivation, that's where.*

*Tempting, but a little too out there for me.*

*Emma toyed with the notion. Was he really too out there? She was tempted, sorely tempted. Her steps slowed.*

*Maybe I should ask him if he'd like to join me for a bite to eat. He does seem kinda lonely.*

*At last she shook her head. No, rein in your wayward libido, girl. He's way too out there for you.*

\* \*

*John trotted up the trail, lagging far enough behind that she wouldn't grow anxious, but still he kept close track of her striking mahogany mane of hair—that silky hair he'd caressed in his dream state. He wanted to touch her again, make certain she was real.*

*Another human being could see him, speak with him. It was a miracle. It had to be. Surely the devil didn't possess such power. Now he understood the meaning of his vision. She was his salvation, his saving grace. Only the heavenly hosts had the power to bring a woman like Emma Rose to Loch Ness.*

*She must have come in one of those flying boats, the big metal birds he'd seen from his mountain home. What were they called? He'd heard passing mention of them over the years. Air planes. Aye, air planes. She'd arrived in an air plane, traveled through the skies all the way from the Colonies.*

*As far as John was concerned that was as much as he needed to know. He didn't have the time or patience to bother with the intricacies of modern travel. The moving horseless carriages that traversed the narrow roadway paralleling the loch were bad enough. They were far beyond his comprehension.*

*The important thing was, she could see him. Nothing else mattered.*

*He watched her enter the back door of a cottage, a cottage he passed daily on his way to the loch. John had never paid much attention before. People came and went, usually couples. They never saw him as he hiked from the mountain to the loch and back again. He never spoke. There was no reason to speak.*

*Why should the dead talk to the living?*

*Because I can, by God.*

*Light glowed from the open door, illuminating the path leading to the entrance of the cottage. John stopped short, afraid to approach any closer. He knew he'd frightened the woman, or at least disconcerted her, but he couldn't help himself. He couldn't turn around and walk away.*

*John stared at the door, stared at her profile as she busied herself in the kitchen. His heart began to pound as he stood stock still in the gloaming.*

*To speak with another person after centuries of silence…*

*It took all his strength to hold back, restrain himself. He wanted to burst through the doorway and fall down on his knees in gratitude. Worship her and what she portended—a possible release from his prison, from this existence that was neither life nor death.*

*If she would but let him grab hold of her, he'd never let her go.*

*Remember, John, ye are a dead man. What can a dead man do with the living?*

*Not a bluidy thing.*

*Yet there was warmth in the gloaming that hadn't been there the day before. It beckoned to him, urged him to stay right where he was, because of her.*

*John felt a stiff lump grow in his throat and he forced himself to walk away from the door, from the light, from the silhouette of this living, breathing, beautiful creature.*

*His unwilling feet took him up the path toward his mountain hideaway, farther and farther from the unexpected reprieve the woman named Emma Rose promised, farther than ever from hope. John's heart grew as cold as the water in the loch and he shivered in the fading light.*

*The dead don't belong with the living.*

\* \* \*

*Emma opened her eyes, confused for a moment by the feel of a strange bed, the sight of an unfamiliar room, the vision of white chintz curtains fluttering in a chill breeze from an open window. Then she remembered.*

*Scotland!*

*Morning had arrived, wet and deliciously misty.*

*Yummy cold air.*

*Emma stretched like a long, lazy cat, feeling more relaxed than she'd felt in years. She'd slept well for a change, burrowed deep within the comfy feather bed.*

*"What time is it?"*

*She lifted herself on her elbows, searching the bedroom for a clock.*

*"I don't think there is a clock."*

*She spotted her cell phone on the bedside table. The thing wouldn't have service unless she was back in Inverness, but at least she could get the correct time. She pressed the on button.*

*"Ten? I slept until ten? I slept fourteen hours? When was the last time...?"*

*Emma couldn't remember the last time she'd slept so late. With a big grin on her face, she plopped back down into the over-stuffed pillows.*

*This feels dang good.*

*Now if only there was a sexy guy with me. Emma snuggled onto her side, hugging an extra pillow. Like that handsome Highlander I met last night.*

*What was his name?*

*"I can'nae remember yer name." She tried to imitate his Scottish brogue and burst into giggles. "The heck I can't. This red-blooded American woman can'nae forget the sight of yer bare chest, John Charles McGregor." She tossed the quilts aside and climbed out of the big four-poster bed. "Wonder which cottage is his. He must be one of my neighbors, not that any of my neighbors live nearby."*

*Emma glanced out the window. The loch was obscured by mist, but she thought she saw a hint of blue peeking through the low clouds. She had big plans today, plans that included a hike to the Falls of Foyers. Emma wasn't about to let a little fog stop her.*

*In fact, she looked forward to it. The cold wet air would feel wonderful. Refreshing. Invigorating.*

*Emma's stomach churned with excitement. This would be her first full day in Scotland.*

*So, let's get going. Shower, breakfast, pack a little lunch. Head off on a mountain adventure. What could be wrong with that?*

*Now where did I put my hiking boots?*

\* \* \*

Emma stopped at a crossroads to study her topo map. She'd made it up the steep ridge above Loch Ness without a problem, and she believed she was headed in the right direction. She'd even stopped at the overlook to catch a brief glimpse of beautiful Urquhardt Castle before it had been swallowed by the mist, but as she'd headed further into the mountains, the sun had disappeared altogether, and the fog had grown so thick she couldn't see more than a few feet in front of her.

"Three hours and not a single sign." Water splattered against the top of her head. Emma glanced up in time to see a squirrel running along the low overhanging branches of a pine tree. He vanished into the fog.

"Great. Just great. Guess I picked the wrong day to hike to the falls." Everything Emma had read about the Highlands had said, be prepared. The weather in the mountains can change from minute to minute.

Well she wasn't prepared. "I'm such an idiot. I'm standing here in a sweater and hiking pants, no jacket, no windbreaker, no hat or gloves and... Ouch! Now what? What's this?" She rubbed her face. Ice crystals stung her cheek. "Sleet? You've got to be kidding me."

Emma blew out a long slow irritated breath. She wasn't mad at Scotland. She wasn't mad at the weather. She was mad at her own impatience. She knew better than to set out on a hike without the proper clothing and equipment.

"Well, honey, you asked for it. Cold weather is what you wanted and cold weather is what you get." Emma turned around and stared back the way she'd come. The fog *was just as thick in that direction. If anything, the visibility was worse now because of the heavy sleet. "I have no choice. I have to backtrack."*

*"Damn it." Too late she remembered something else she'd read in one of her travel books: Many people die in the mountains in Scotland because they don't think of Scotland as a wild place.*

*"It has to do with quickly changing weather conditions and steep rocky terrain, you dummy."*

*Emma started back down the trail. She was soaked to the skin in no time flat. In good weather it was a three-hour hike, but this was a treacherous slog. The visibility was so poor she couldn't be sure she was heading in the right direction and she was getting colder by the minute. The trail, when she could find it through the growing blanket of sleet, was as slick as an ice-skating rink.*

*When she felt the bite of the wind clear through her wool sweater and her undershirt, she realized she was in big trouble. Her nose felt frozen. Her ears stung with cold. Her hair was plastered to her head in matted curls.*

*Teeth chattering, feet slipping in the muck, Emma skidded over a moss-covered rock and slid down the muddy trail on her back, coming to rest in a wet heap. She stared up at the swirling mist, sleet stinging her eyes. "I'm gonna die up here. My first full day in Scotland and I'm gonna die."*

*"The hell ye are, ye bluidy fool."*

*"What?" Emma recognized the voice. She leaned her head back, looking at him*

*upside down. "What are you doing here?"*

*He didn't answer her question. Instead he wrapped his arms around her and hauled her to her feet. "Can ye stand?"*

*Emma nodded, but he kept a firm grip on her anyway.*

*"Ye must be mad to come out in such a downpour. Ye could have ended up over that cliff." He pointed off to her right, gesturing toward a stand of trees almost completely obscured by the mist and rain. "'Tis but a few steps further."*

*Emma pulled her hand from his and tried to shove the hair from her eyes. "I don't... I don't understand. Where did you come from?" She shivered so bad her knees shook. "I'm cold," she said.*

*"Aye, I can see that." He looked her up and down. "Come."*

*"Huh?" Her teeth were chattering again. "Come where?"*

*"Come wi' me." He held out his hand. "Come. I will'nae hurt ye."*

*Cold as she was, Emma still had the wherewithal to search his wide green eyes for any malicious intent. She sensed she could trust him. She concluded that while the man might be eccentric, he was an innocent. He meant her no harm. At least that's what her gut said. She shook her wet hair and straightened her shoulders. "Okay, it's not like I have a choice, I guess."*

*His big warm hand surrounded her ice-cold fist. "Oh, ye always have a choice, lass. The trick is to make the right choice. Ye are making the right choice."*

\* \* \*

*Halfway to his rock hideaway the woman's legs gave out. John caught her before he fell, face first, into the mud. Without hesitation he slung her pack over his back and lifted her limp form into his arms. He carried her through the freezing rain. The downpour, the mist and the limited visibility didn't slow him. He could make his way over the entire mountain blindfolded. After all, he'd trod its pathways daily for nearly three hundred years and the cold had no effect on him. The woman in his arms, on the other hand, was soaked to the skin and suffering from exposure to the elements.*

*The Highlands were a deceptively cruel place. Always had been, always would be. The harsh weather was made for those with a hardy constitution. The elements had no special regard for the softer town folk. When he'd seen her leave her cottage in the morning, prepared to hike off into the mountains, he'd followed, hoping for an opportunity to speak with her again. But he hadn't expected her to try to kill herself.*

*God in heaven, wet and bedraggled as she was, John couldn't ignore the softness of her skin beneath his fingertips any more than he could help the fact that his hand had slid beneath her dripping sweater; that his fingers burned where they touched bare skin.*

*The woman was too thin. John shook his head. If he chose to, he could count her ribs. Women in his day had carried some meat on their bones. But it had been so long since he'd been this close to any other human being, let alone a woman...*

*She made him feel... John wasn't certain how he felt. The weight of this Emma in his arms, no matter how slight, made him remember, made him want the impossible—something he hadn't considered in years, a life.*

*He held another human being in his arms. He carried her to safety.*

*How is this possible?*

*'Tis'nae possible. But be grateful just the same. She might be dead if not for ye.*

*Gratitude? Perhaps fear would be the saner reaction.*

*John felt a great deal of both. His ability to interact with her made no sense.*

*Unless ye have remained behind for a single reason, to save the life of this one woman.*

*He stopped in his tracks, the rain and wind lashing his face. It was the only explanation that made any sense.*

*So, save her, man.*

*He pressed her even closer, the chill of her seeping through him as if he were still alive, as if he could feel the cold. He plowed ahead through the mud and the wet, hurrying to his shelter.*

*He needed to get her dry and warm. He wished he had something in the way of sustenance to offer her, but he had nothing. He didn't require food or drink. He felt the slight weight of her pack on his back. Perhaps she'd brought some food with her although she certainly hadn't thought to carry warm clothing.*

*John shook the wet strands of hair from his eyes. Only a quarter mile remained between the two of them and safety.*

\* \* \*

"What is this?" Emma pulled the worn wool blanket away from her face. It smelled of wood smoke and man.

"'Tis a plaid."

"A plaid?"

"Aye. 'Tis my hunting plaid."

"Why is it on me?"

He cleared his throat. "T'was all I had."

"All you had for what?" She peeked beneath the plaid. Her eyes opened wide.
"Where are my clothes?"

He jerked his head. "There. Drying by the fire." He carefully placed another log
into the flames.

Jeez Louise. He's seen me naked. Emma opened her mouth to protest but nothing
came out. He saved your life. Shut up. "What happened to me?"

"Ye were caught out in inclement weather." He shrugged. "A common enough
occurrence here in the mountains."

Emma squinted and looked him over from head to toe. He'd removed his leather
boots, but his hair was dripping wet and his clothes clung to him. "But you're soaked
too. You...? How did you...? Were you following me?"

Instead of answering her, he turned back to the fire. "Now that ye are awake, I
must find some dry clothing for myself."

"Uh, here?" Emma looked around. "You have clothing here? It's a, a cave. We're
in a cave." She felt around, trying to discover where he'd put her. "This is a rock

ledge." She pulled up a wad of fabric, blankets; odd articles of clothing. Her eyes opened wide. "Is this your bed?"

"Aye." He loomed above her. "And ye are sitting upon my dry garments."

Emma had never felt so flustered in her entire life. Clutching the blanket, or hunting plaid, or whatever he'd called it, she tried to move off his clothes.

She scooted over, but a corner of the blanket caught under her hip and the fabric tore from her grasp.

A shock of cold air hit her bare chest. Emma's head flew up. He stared at her breasts, stared with such a naked look of fierce hunger and gut deep longing that Emma didn't know whether to scream in embarrassment or thrust her chest forward to give him a better view.

She did neither. She sat perfectly still, but that didn't stop her nipples from puckering into tight little buds, nor did her lack of movement prevent a sudden and unexpected warmth from pooling right between her legs.

Emma's stomach turned crazy somersaults. She was aroused. She knew it and she knew he knew it. Her cheeks grew flaming hot and she felt the flush spread over her neck and her chest, all the way down to her bellybutton.

His eyes narrowed as he perused her. The green pupils darkened to an emerald flame. The rise and fall of his chest quickened. He opened and closed his fists.

Then he growled. The man named John Charles McGregor literally growled at her.

"Do ye mean to torture me, woman? 'Tis painful enough..." He didn't finish his *sentence. Instead he grabbed her soggy sweater and tossed it in her direction before he turned his back to her, stomping the few feet across the rock floor to stand in the entrance to the cave.*

*Emma stared at his back.*

*What the hell?*

*She tried to shove her arms into the sleeves, but the sweater was too wet and sticky.*

*"Ewww. Itches. I'm not putting this on." She risked a quick look at him. He still had his back turned to her. His wet clothes outlined every muscle across his torso.*

*Damn, the man is pure man candy.*

*She made sure the blanket was wrapped tight around her shoulders before she rose from her rocky perch. "Here, I'll move and you can get your dry clothes, as long as you don't mind if I keep your blanket, uh, I mean your hunting plaid for now." Her legs shook, and she stumbled, the uneven stone floor abrading the soggy soles of her feet. "I feel like a wrinkled old prune."*

*He brushed past her and rifled through his clothes, apparently looking for something dry. "Ye are nae wrinkled, nor old, and I hae ne'er tasted a prune."*

*"You've never tasted...? Wait a minute." Emma tried and failed to suppress a grin. "Are you flirting with me?"*

*He lifted his head. "Flirting wi' ye?" He appeared confused by the word. "Ah, ye mean a seduction?" For the first time since she'd encountered him, John flashed a spontaneous, unguarded smile. "The thought did cross my mind."*

*The words were spoken in a low voice, but Emma heard him loud and clear. Her mouth fell open.*

*He slid a finger under her chin and closed her mouth. "Aye, ye hae nice white teeth; I noticed when I encountered ye at the loch yesterday eve."*

*In one quick motion, he drew the wet linen shirt over his head, exposing about as much excellent beefcake as Emma had ever seen in her life. She felt like fanning herself but if she did, she'd probably drop her blanket, uh, plaid, again.*

*He leaned nearer the fire to shake some of the remaining water from his long, brown hair. Emma could only stare.*

*He straightened up and smiled at her, the corners of his eyes crinkling in a very appealing way. "The thought of a seduction has'nae occurred to me in many a year. It would nae hae been possible in any case. Ye hae nary a notion of what it is to be invisible."*

*"You? Invisible? That's hard to believe. I'm sure every woman for miles around these parts has noticed you. You're hard to miss."*

*The smile vanished, but so did the rock-hard abs as he pulled on a dry shirt.*

*Emma sighed with regret, but her eyes remained glued to his chest. "Your clothes are certainly old-fashioned. Nobody wears shirts like that anymore. Shirts that tie at the neck, I mean." She clutched his plaid with one hand and reached for the cuff of his sleeve, running her finger over the edge. "Is that hand-sewn embroidery?"*

*"Aye." His voice was as muted as the light in the cavern.*

He held his wrist still before the golden glow of the fire, as if he savored the touch of her hand and Emma found herself wondering just how long it had been since John Charles McGregor had been touched, by anyone.

"Where'd you buy it?"

"Buy it?"

"Yes. What store?"

"Store?"

Emma cleared her throat, shifting the plaid higher up her shoulders. "I guess we have a language barrier. I mean a shop. Which shop sells these hand-embroidered shirts?"

He pulled his arm away and began to search through the pile of clothes for a pair of dry trousers. "I din'nae buy it in a shop."

A switch in Emma's brain clicked on. She'd read about Japanese soldiers from World War II still hiding in caves forty, fifty years after the war. Maybe he was... What? Hiding out? And if so, he'd been hiding out for some time. But he was young. She studied his face. John Charles McGregor couldn't be more than thirty years old.

His speech was antiquated. His clothes appeared equally antique, straight out of a Scottish Highlander romance novel. The shirt looked like it was made of homespun linen and there were no buttons, no collar, just a tie at the neck.

She noticed he'd left it untied, which exposed a nice triangle of bare skin. It was very distracting.

*"Turn around, lass."*

*Emma blinked. "Huh?"*

*"I wish to put on some dry trousers, but yer starin' at my chest, lassie. Turn around unless ye wish to see more of me than ye have already." It was impossible to miss the amusement in his voice and the challenge in his words.*

*"I don't think so." Emma felt uncharacteristically bold. She allowed the plaid to slide off one bare shoulder. "Turnabout is fair play. You've seen me naked."*

*He stood stock still and stared at her, one hand frozen on the buttons of his wet trousers, the other hand holding the dry pair.*

*Emma couldn't help it. She eyed the buttons. "These are really old." She stepped closer, running a light finger over the top button. "These are so old, these brass buttons. I've seen them in antique stores."*

*Before she realized what she was doing, Emma felt his body respond to her touch. She sucked in a breath and withdrew her hand. "Sorry." But her eyes never moved. She wanted to see him. A fire burned deep in her belly, a smoldering she hadn't felt in ages. Her nipples tingled all over again. She thrust her shoulders back, met his eyes.*

*"It is only fair. You removed my clothes."*

*Oh my god, what are you doing, Emma? Get a grip.*

*Get a grip on what? Against Emma's will, her eyes traveled down again. Get a grip on his rather impressive male attribute?*

*"I believe ye are flirting wi' me, lassie." He unbuttoned the top button.*

*Emma tried to look away.*

*He unbuttoned the second button.*

*"I'm sorry. I shouldn't have challenged you. I don't even know you." Emma tore her eyes from him and spun around, only to find herself staring at his flame-kissed shadow on the rock wall. "Oh god." She stepped on the plaid and lost her grip, felt it slip down her back. She tried to grab for it, but it slid over her bottom, down her legs, and pooled about her feet.*

*"Lass…"*

*That single word spoken in a rough masculine whisper sent shivers racing up and down her spine.*

*I could have a vacation fling with a complete stranger and no one would be the wiser.*

*"I want ye, lass." His warm breath tickled her ear. "Ye are the most beautiful sight these eyes hae seen in near to three hundred years, but I can'nae…" She felt him run the pads of his fingers along her shoulder and her legs grew weak. "I will'nae take advantage of a woman in distress."*

*Emma forced her voice to work. "I'm not in distress."*

*He nudged her hair aside with his chin.*

*Emma resisted a powerful urge to turn into his body.*

*His lips brushed the back of her neck and she began to shake.*

\* \* \*

*"Aye," he said, "but I am in great distress." John tried to resist the seductive spicy scent of her hair, but he failed. His lips brushed the tender skin of her neck.*

*One taste of her rain-kissed skin was enough to kill him all over again. Emma Rose, a woman of this time, was both an innocent and a temptress. She was a wicked blade thrust into his side and twisted with a vengeance.*

*She was not for him.*

*Yet he stood so close the warmth of her naked body warmed his own. He felt alive for the first time in... He could no longer remember how long he'd been dead.*

*Chill bumps rose on her exposed flesh.*

*"Ye are cold." He bent down, caught the edge of his plaid, but before he could wrap the worn woolen around her, she turned. Her nipples brushed his chest, sending a slice of wild fire through his entire body. He was hard as a rock in an instant.*

*John dropped the plaid. "Bluidy hell, woman, I may be dead but I am no' a saint."*

*His took her in his arms and pulled her close. Those lips, those soft rose red lips of hers demanded a good hard kissing and her body cried out for even more. John wanted to be the man to give it to her, give her every inch. But he hesitated.*

*He was dead. She was alive. To kiss her would be sacrilege. Or something akin to it.*

*John pushed her away. He realized his action seemed brusque, but he needed to put some space between them before he did something both of them would regret. He reached down for his plaid and wrapped it around her shoulders.*

He saw the hurt in her eyes, the rejection written all over her face. It occurred to John she'd had experience with rejection. Perhaps not so long ago.

He tried to explain. "'Tis no' ye, lass. 'Tis me. Ye must be one of the fae," he muttered. "Surely ye've cast a spell over me."

"Fae?" Her voice was nothing more than a whisper.

"The faery people."

"You mean the little people, like leprechauns?"

"No." John smiled at the word. "Ye are no a leprechaun. More like a fae princess." He guided her back to the ledge. "Sit, warm yerself. When yer clothes are dry I will lead ye back to the cottage."

"I'm sorry," she said. She seemed confused. Then she straightened her shoulders. "It must be the cold. That's the only explanation. Or I'm dreaming, or something. I don't…" He watched the muscles in her neck contract as she swallowed, hard. She shoved a few wet strands of hair from her cheek. He saw the flame there, the rosy blush kissing her pale face. "I don't throw myself at men. I've never thrown myself at a man. I haven't been with a man in… No man has touched me like that for…" And then she shut her mouth, tightened her hold on his plaid, and sat down. "I don't know why I'm even… You must think I'm a… Well, you must think I'm an awful person."

John rubbed his forehead. No, he didn't think she was an awful person. He thought she was a goddess, but he was every bit as confused as she. John sat down beside her. He wanted to take her hand, but she clutched at his plaid, held it so tight to her throat *her knuckles had turned white.*

*"Nay. Dun'nae fash yerself, lass. Ye are suffering from cold and I am suffering from…" John stopped talking and sat beside her. He cleared his throat. "'Tis lonely here in these mountains. It has been many a year since I hae spoken wi' one such as yerself."*

*"Why not?"*

*"I am dead." The words escaped his mouth before he could bite them back.*

*Emma burst out laughing. "You're not dead. I mean, sometimes loneliness makes us feel dead. I know the feeling. I understand loneliness." She blew out a big breath. "I was married for five years, but it felt like I was all alone. Every single day. I understand what you're saying, but you're not dead." She loosened her grip on his plaid, reached a hand out to him and gave him a tentative pat on the knee. "Sometimes it feels like you're dead, but really, it's not so bad. Look at me. Here I am, in Scotland. I may be lost and cold and naked, but I'm in Scotland." She lifted her eyes. "I'm babbling, aren't I? Sorry."*

*John smiled. "I could listen to ye babble on all day. Yer voice gives me great pleasure." He studied his meager campsite. "I wish I could offer ye something, some food. I have nothing, not a morsel."*

*She followed his eyes, studying his poor excuse for a home. He could only imagine what she must think of him. Then she turned those perceptive eyes back to him. "Where do you get your food? Do you get, uh, handouts? Is there a homeless shelter* nearby?"

"A homeless shelter?"

"Yes," she said. "You know, a place where people like you, people without a home can get something to eat and drink and maybe find a warm bed."

"I am nae homeless."

"Well, if you're not homeless, um, what do you call this? Is this your home?"

"Nay."

"Where's your home? Do you live in one of the cottages near the lake, I mean loch?"

John shook his head. "My home was on an isle near to Skye. We lived under The MacLeod of Raasay."

"Was?"

"Aye. Was."

"But it's not now?"

"It has'nae been for a long time, not since I was thirty years of age."

She squinted her eyes. "And how old are you now?"

"Do ye truly wish to know?"

She nodded. Grinned at him. "Sure. Unless it's some big state secret."

"Are ye certain ye wish to know?"

"Of course. I'll go first if it makes you feel less self-conscious. I'm twenty-nine. There's no need to be so mysterious."

*"Aye, lass, there is indeed. If I tell ye, ye may run off and fall over a cliff."*

*Emma laughed at his words. "Don't be silly, John Charles McGregor of Raasay. I'm not going to run off willy-nilly in this pea soup fog."*

*"I hae haunted these mountains for two hundred and seventy years so I am supposing that would make me three hundred years old."*

\* \* \*

*Emma choked. If she'd had a mouthful of water, she'd have spit it out all over the stone floor.*

*He pounded her on the back.*

*She put up a hand. "Stop. I'm okay."*

*Holy smokes. Here she was, wet, naked, wrapped in a plaid that smelled of pure unadulterated man, sitting next to the sexiest thing, make that Highlander, she'd ever seen in her entire life, not that she'd ever seen a Highlander before in person, but still... Here she was sitting next to the sexiest Highland beast in all creation and he was crazy as a loon. Not dangerous. Just, to quote him, bluidy insane.*

*She turned to John Charles McGregor. "Let me get this straight."*

*"Straight?"*

*Of course. Emma decided to humor him. "It's an expression. It means, let me be clear. You're telling me that you're a ghost, a three-hundred-year-old ghost."*

*"Aye."*

*"Huh."*

"That is all ye hae to say on the subject?" He blinked at her, blinked those dark emerald green eyes at her. Oh, there were depths in those eyes. Emma couldn't miss the depths. A woman could drown in such deep and dangerous waters. An image of the mysterious depths of Loch Ness flashed through Emma's brain.

"Well, I will say one thing for ye, lass. Ye appear to be taking the news a might better than I did." He seemed to study her. "Ye don'nae intend to swoon, do ye?"

Swoon? On you? I'd love to swoon on you, crazy or no.

And that makes me bluidy crazy for sure.

"No," Emma said. "I'm not the swooning type." The plaid had slipped down her shoulder and she saw him staring at her bare skin. The hungry look had returned in force.

"Hey, you know what? I have some food in my backpack."

He continued to stare at her shoulder. Emma cleared her throat. "My backpack?" She stuck out a hand so she could point. "Over there? Food?"

He seemed to shake himself. He glanced into her eyes again. "I don'nae eat."

"Ah, right. Ghost. Well, I do." Emma rose to her feet, bringing the plaid with her this time. "I bet I can convince you to eat something. I've packed some terrific sandwiches. And strawberries. I picked up the sweetest little strawberries at the store in Inverness." She turned back to look at him. "I'm rambling again, aren't I?"

John shrugged. "I relish the sound of yer voice."

He proceeded to smile a smile so filled with warmth and longing, Emma flushed *from the top of her head to the ends of her toes.*

*"Feel free to ramble as much as ye wish, lass. I am sure ye hae verra sweet little strawberries." He sat back, crossed his arms over that manly chest, and leaned against the rock wall, making himself comfortable, settling in for a long gab fest. Or a night of pure debauchery. Emma wasn't sure which.*

*But if she had to choose, she'd choose debauchery first, gab fest second. Wait, verra verra sweet little strawberries? Oh yeah. Definitely debauchery. Said strawberries tingled in anticipation.*

*"Here." She tried to keep the quiver out of her voice as she sat back down beside him and opened her pack. "Sandwiches." Her hand shook as she unwrapped the simple fare. "It's just bread and cheese, a little mustard. And, um, strawberries."*

*She placed one of the strawberries in the palm of her free hand. "Here."*

*He stared at the berry like it was poisonous.*

*"You've eaten strawberries before, right?"*

*"Aye."*

*"Soooooo, have one now. I'm offering you my berries."*

*Oh my god, did I just say that?*

*He dropped his eyes. They fixed on her chest. His grin was positively wicked. "Aye. I can see that, lass."*

*Emma followed his gaze. "Oh." The blanket, uh, plaid, had slipped again. Her body seemed determined to fight her. Her body wanted him. Her mind screamed—*

*lunatic!*

*Either he's a lunatic or you're a lunatic. The last thing you need is a Highland fling with a lunatic! And he probably isn't packing condoms anywhere in this cave of his.*

*Emma decided to call him on his outlandish claim. She blew out a breath. "If you're a ghost, disappear."*

*His eyes remained riveted on her breasts. His hands were tucked under his arms like he was desperate to stop himself from reaching for her, but at last he shook himself, and he lifted his head.*

*This time it was Emma who couldn't take her eyes off his body, specifically the prominent bulge in the front of his wool trousers.*

*"What did ye say, lass?" His voice was as thick as the mist swirling about the entrance to the cave.*

*There was no way he could disguise his yearning and, lord help her, Emma felt exactly the same. She moved then, almost without conscious thought, drawing her free arm over her breasts as if trying to remove temptation. The other hand still stuck out in his direction, holding the strawberry. Emma gazed at the hand, in a vacant sort of way, and wondered if that arm of hers had turned to stone. For a second even her voice stuck in her throat, but only for a second.*

*"I said, if you're a ghost, disappear."*

*He did.*

*Emma's mouth fell open. The strawberry slipped from her hand. She watched it drop, as if in slow motion, to the floor of the cave. In the silence that followed his sudden absence she swore she could hear the infinitesimally tiny sound of its berrylicious plop.*

*I'm losing my mind.*

*"Come back," she whispered, her heart pounding. "Please, come back, John Charles McGregor."*

*All six feet plus of said John Charles McGregor materialized before her.*

*Emma remembered to bring the plaid with her when she rose to her feet. She faced him, stood so close his warm breath brushed her forehead. Her voice shook. "Do it again."*

*And he was gone.*

*Just. Like. That.*

*Goosebumps rose over her entire body. Emma's knees felt a little weak and for a few seconds she considered fainting, but then something occurred to her.*

*"I know what this is. I'm dying. I'm not in a cave. I'm out there in the rain and the sleet and the fog and I'm dying of hypothermia. And this is a hypothermic hallucination. I'm probably taking my last breath right now. It's the only logical explanation."*

*She heard his disembodied voice. "Nay, lass. I am the only logical explanation."*

*And there he was, standing in front of her once again, but this time he took her in his big strong arms and lifted her up, lifted her so he could press his lips against hers for a kiss.*

*And not just any kiss. His was an unforgettable kiss, a kiss for the ages. A kiss that seared her, scorched her, burned a hole clear through her chest wall, all the way into her aching, painful, broken heart.*

*He had her with that kiss. Emma melted into the dead Mr. McGregor's kiss, all the pain of her failed marriage, the loss of her babies, the end of her career, was forgotten, vanished, poof, the same way he'd vanished from her sight.*

*For once in her life she dropped her guard. Emma, Miss Control Freak, became a creature of pure biology. Her body understood one thing and one thing only—I want to experience this big hard man. The word control did not enter into the equation.*

*John Charles McGregor took up her entire field of vision. His mere presence erased any concerns about whether he was a hallucination or dead.*

*She stood safe within his arms and he felt as alive as any man she'd ever known.*

*No, Emma corrected herself. She had never known a man like this. John Charles McGregor felt like the only man alive in the whole wide world.*

*How could she do this? Do something so raw, so primitive? So... So out of her comfort zone, to say the least.*

*Or maybe I should say, to say the most—something so out of control?*

*Because she could. There was nothing to stand in her way and no one to stop her. For the first time in years Emma was her own woman and she could choose.*

*She chose him.*

\*  \*  \*

*John struggled to make sense of his overwhelming desire for Emma Rose, not because he didn't understand desire, there was no question in his mind about that, he understood desire very well, but because a ghost shouldn't feel. Or couldn't feel. Yet the blood rushed through his veins so fast, the pounding of his heart was so loud, he could barely hear himself think.*

*She embodied everything he had craved for nearly three hundred years. It was not only companionship that he'd lacked, it was the tenderness of a woman. There was no denying that Emma was real flesh and blood beneath his hands, warm to the touch. No, not merely warm, she burned. Her heat set his body and soul aflame.*

*For one night, at least, John decided to rejoin the land of the living because by some miracle this woman, this Emma Rose, made it possible.*

*He sat on the rocky ledge that passed for a bed, and he ran his hands up and down her bare thighs, creating even more heat. It was enough to kill a living man. John had lingered too long in solitude. He could not wait any longer.*

*He lifted Emma onto his lap so that she straddled him, palming her breasts as he did so, running his thumbs over her perfect pink nipples. She didn't resist, no, on the contrary. She moaned with pleasure, her eager hands already on those brass buttons she had previously praised.*

*Her lips never left his as she guided him inside.*

*John lost his heart and soul at the feel of her, the bare heat of her. He felt home for the first time in centuries. He wondered if the feeling would last, but the wonder was fleeting for he was soon consumed by Emma, in the passion, in the joy of possessing and being possessed. He was a man with a woman. It mattered not a whit that she was a stranger to him.*

*It mattered not a whit that he was dead.*

*Soon she was no stranger. He knew Emma Rose in the most intimate way possible. And that was all he knew.*

\* \* \*

*Emma buried her face in John's shoulder, seeking protection from her own thoughts.*

*"I can't believe what just happened, twice," she whispered. "I've never felt anything…" She couldn't finish her sentence.*

*"Aye."*

*The word was more like a breath than speech. He said nothing else, but he stroked her bare arm, used his other hand to brush the tousled hair from her forehead. Even this gentle touch aroused her.*

*She had discovered that John Charles McGregor was much man.*

*Oh, but he's not a man. Is he?*

*Emma lifted her head. "What are you, John, really?"*

*"Too soon, Emma Rose. I don'nae wish to talk about what I am and what I am*

*not. I hae spent near to three hundred years trying to ascertain what I am and am not."*

*He sat up, pulling her with him. He leaned his back against the rough rock wall, keeping her between his legs so she could rest against his broad chest. "I hae no wish to return to that dark place right now, no' with ye so alive in my arms."*

*Oh, I do believe I've just entered Swoonville... "John?"*

*"Aye?" His fingers toyed with her erect nipples.*

*"Make love to me again."*

*He turned her head towards his so their lips could meet. She felt his smile as he kissed her.*

*"Aye, lassie. With pleasure."*

\* \* \*

*Secure in John's strong arms, a toasty warm and utterly sated Emma drifted in a post-amorous semi-sleep. She registered the light of the fire through half-closed eyes. It was the only illumination in the rocky alcove, but she didn't mind her primitive surroundings. Somehow the surroundings made everything better. To be here in this wild place with this wild man, or un-man, or whatever he was, made everything just right.*

*In any case, darkness had descended, bringing along with it an ice-cold deluge. There would be no hike down to her cottage tonight.*

*Not that the cold or the rain mattered. She felt safe and protected, even cherished. Perish the thought!*

*Emma realized it was the first time in ages she'd felt safe with a man. Maybe she didn't know who or what John Charles McGregor was, but she knew he was a good man.*

*She dozed, barely aware of the storm, wrapped tight in John's warmth.*

*He cleared his throat and began to speak, but the words were muted by the rain and a sleepy Emma strained to hear. Mostly she listened through the vibrations in his chest. It seemed easier that way, and she got the distinct impression John wanted to speak without an obvious audience. He didn't want comments or sympathy or even eye contact.*

*She realized he just wanted to get it said, whatever it was.*

*So, Emma closed her eyes and listened.*

*"I din'nae want to go, to do battle wi' the English. I had new a wife, ye see. We had barely grown accustomed to living wi' each other and she had just given birth. A boy. The bairn was a boy. My first son, my only child, James Alexander McGregor.*

*"But I am a Scot and worse, a McGregor. The government of England has ne'er been a friend to Clan McGregor."*

*Emma had read something about that, something about Clan McGregor being banned or outlawed, hunted down and slaughtered, but she held her peace and let John continue his tale without interruption.*

*"We received word the bonny prince had landed in Scotia. It was'nae the happy news ye might expect. Unlike the stories ye may hae heard, he was'nae welcomed wi'*

*open arms by one and all. The uprising during the time of my father and grandfather had caused much suffering among the clans. Many of us had no wish for more of the same, or worse. Some of the clans were aligned wi' the English in any case. Times had changed, ye see. They din'nae care to see a restoration of the Stuart monarchy.*

*"But enthusiasm grew. It does among men. There is a need to test one's mettle. A desire to right old wrongs, especially for Clan Gregor. But still, I din'nae want to go."*
*He sighed. "Yet go I did. We met up with Prince Charles in Edinburgh, fought with him at Falkirk, but then retreated to Inverness and Fort Augustus. We awaited the French; we were promised reinforcements, supplies, weapons. They ne'er arrived.*

*"The English, under Cumberland, made camp and o'er-wintered. They were rested, well-supplied; well-fed, reinforced by the Hessians. They possessed artillery. We carried broadswords, dirks, pikes, staves. We marched all night, two nights, three, those that were left of us after Prestonpas, to reach Drummossie Moor. In the rain, in the sleet, in the cold. Some of the men walked on boots held together wi' rags. The leather soles had worn through after months of hard use.*

*"I journeyed with my brothers, my uncles, my cousins, my friends. We fought with the Duke of Perth's regiment, under John Drummond, Master of Strathallan.*

*"We engaged the English and such Highland clans who supported the Crown, the lowlanders and the Hessians. The battle was brief, nae more than an hour. One would think such a battle should last days, a battle that changed the face of the Highlands fore'er. Ye ken?"*

*Emma didn't answer. John fell quiet, lay still for a long time. She waited, patient. She knew from the sound of his breathing he hadn't fallen asleep.*

*"T'was suicide. T'was reckless and courageous and terrible and beautiful and bluidy suicide. I fought my way through a bog only to be separated from my men, from my family. Most died, killed by the cannon fire or cut down by the Redcoats. Any survivors were taken prisoner to be hanged soon after.*

*"At last I crawled to the top of a rise. I caught site of the Prince upon his horse far away from the battlefield. He could'nae e'en see his army from where he sat. I watched him turn and flee wi' his guards close behind. I knew all was lost so I did the same as he. I had fought my way well beyond Cumberland's line. The rain fell, the mist descended, and the light was fading. I saw an opening and I ran wi' nothing more than my sword and my dirk and the clothes on my back. I got as far as these mountains.*

*"I could'nae get home to Raasay. Not wi' the Butcher's men about, raiding, stealing, burning every croft, leaving the women and children to starve.*

*"There may hae been others like me. I dun'nae know. I had no food. The weather was foul. The roads were filled with Redcoats hunting survivors and stragglers and anything else that moved. I had nae other choice but to hide in these mountains. I din'nae last long, a month, no more."*

*His voice held no emotion. Emma felt as if she listened to a recitation, or a reading, or a simple statement of fact. Terrible fact.*

*But there was power in that simplicity, far more power than if he'd beaten his breast or sobbed or cried or screamed or pleaded for her belief and understanding. John did none of these things. His simple eloquence provided enough drama.*

*Emma knew he didn't want to see her reaction, to have to react to her reaction. He wanted nothing more than to tell his story.*

*Then he said, "I din'nae do what I could to protect my family. I din'nae do enough. A man should protect those in his care. A man should be responsible for the lives of his family."*

*He fell silent again.*

*Emma said, "It wasn't your fault. You didn't have a choice." She knew from the dismissive sound he made that he disagreed with her.*

*"I told ye a'fore. One always has a choice. The trick is to make the right choice. I din'nae make the right choice."*

*Oh yeah, when I was out in the cold, dying…*

*"Did you see your family again? I mean, as a ghost? Did you see them?"*

*"Once."*

*"And what happened?"*

*He pressed his cheek to hers. "I could'nae speak wi' them. Could'nae touch them. I tried in vain. And then I was drawn back here, back to this place. T'was nae my choice that time."*

*"You never saw your family again, never heard anything about them?"*

*"Nay."*

*"You don't know what happened to them?"*

*"Nay, lass. Leave off. 'Tis nothing to be done now. They were buried long ago."*

*Emma wondered if she could learn what had happened to his family. She opened her mouth to say as much, but she closed it again. She found herself as reluctant to talk about it as he was.*

*Would I want to know?*

*Emma knew the answer. It was a resounding, no. "What can I do to help?"*

*She listened to the pounding of his heart, waited for his response.*

*"Will ye gi' me yer woman's heat, yer warmth? Mayhap 'tis oblivion I seek, the cessation of pain, the soothing of dark memories. My mind goes quiet when I make love with ye, lass. 'Tis a better remedy than skipping pebbles in the loch."*

*Emma pressed a kiss into the side of his neck. She felt dampness, a dampness she knew for certain had been left by a trail of tears.*

*"Are ye willing to gi' yerself to me once again?" His voice sounded, for lack of a better word, wistful.*

*Without hesitation Emma slid on top of him. She studied the rough masculine lines of his face. What a desolate yet beautiful face it was. Here was a man worthy of his sex. Emma knew deep in her bones he was a man with whom she could fall in love. "I'll give myself to you as often as you wish, John Charles McGregor."*

*Before, their lovemaking had been urgent, almost violent, so great was the need for human touch. This time, Emma made certain their lovemaking was sweet, as sweet as she could make it, for his sake. And who knew sweet better than a pastry chef?*

*Who?*

*Emma was willing to bet good money that not another soul in the Highlands understood the definition of sweet, all things sweet, in the same way she did. She would take his pain, sugarcoat it if necessary. Her own pain was nothing in comparison. Nothing. And to think, he'd lived with it for nearly three hundred years.*

*John Charles McGregor must be an incredibly strong man. I couldn't do it; not like he has. I'd have gone insane a couple hundred years ago.*

\* \* \*

*It was near dawn when Emma's empty stomach reached the end of its rope. Her hunger refused to be denied.*

*John lifted his head and grinned.*

*Oh, his grin is so winning. Makes me tingle from head to toe.*

*"I must apologize. I can'nae provide for ye."*

*"No worries," she said, and she reached for her pack. "I can provide for ye."*

*He laughed at her attempted mimicry. "Ye would hae made a good Scot."*

*"I doubt it," Emma said. "Spanish I can handle. Gaelic? Probably not." She opened her backpack and pulled out a full paper bag. "Cheese, bread, strawberries, a bottle of water. I brought food, remember? Oh, I hope you don't think tomatoes are poisonous, because they are not. I put tomatoes on the sandwiches."*

*"Tomatoes?"*

*"Aye, John Charles McGregor. Tomatoes."*

*"I don'nae know if I can eat yer provisions, tomatoes or no."*

*"Well..."* Emma raised her eyebrows. *"We'll never know until we try. Okay, so what do you say we get set up?"*

*"Set up?"*

*She looked down at his naked body and then into his expressive green eyes. "Set up as in we cover certain parts of our bodies as we eat so as not to get distracted by said certain parts."*

*John burst into laughter. It was a glorious sound and it echoed through the cave. Emma laughed with him, knowing full well he probably hadn't laughed in, oh, a few hundred years. She no longer believed she was suffering from hypothermia or dying or hallucinating. A hallucination couldn't, she had to mentally excuse the expression, fuck your brains out.*

*And her brains were definitely out.*

*So there.*

*They sat on the ledge piled with John's rag tag clothing and blankets, or rather, Emma reminded herself, plaids. John placed her upon his thighs and wrapped them both in his hunting plaid. It was that gesture, that simple quiet gesture that reminded her of the depths of John's loneliness.*

*It made her heart hurt. He made her heart hurt.*

*She reached for his hand. Twined her fingers with his. Where would he go? What would he do when she left Scotland? How long would he be forced to haunt the mountains all alone?*

*Emma had a month to spend with him. She would think of something.*

*Then it occurred to her, he was a ghost. If nothing else, she could bring him home with her.*

*I'm not leaving him alone, and that's that. Yes. I'll bring him to the States, so take that, unholy spirits. He's coming home with me.*

*But what if he doesn't like America? And what happens when I...? When I'm not around anymore, what happens to him then?*

*But I can't leave him here all alone.*

*She looked down at their hands, his big masculine, calloused, sword-wielding hand holding her slender feminine long-fingered, piano-playing, cookie-baking hand.*

*I will not leave him alone. I can't do it.*

*Emma covered her dark thoughts with a smile. "Let's eat," she said. She tore a sandwich in half. "I'd like to know what you think of my tomatoes."*

*John grinned from ear to ear. "Are ye referring to yer tomatoes or yer strawberries? Ye already know how much I like yer strawberries. But I think I like yer tomatoes equally well."*

*He is a quick one. Emma laughed. That he is indeed.*

\* \* \*

*It was a fine day. A perfect day in the Highlands. The air had cleared, the sun rose* bright, the dark waters of Loch Ness sparkled with a brilliant iridescent fire in the dawn.

John had dressed in his kilt and his best shirt, which was to say his least threadbare shirt. It wasn't much but it was clean. His boots were still presentable, which was something. He'd slid his dirk into its sheath because a Highlander was not a Highlander without his knife.

He carried his broadsword because Emma had asked him to carry it. She found it fascinating, especially the McGregor crest etched into the hilt with the clan motto: 'S rioghal mo dhream, my race is royal. He'd explained to her that the McGregor clan claimed descent from the ancient kings of Scotland.

His chest felt broader this morning than it had the morning before. Was it because he'd found reason to take pride in his heritage or because Emma Rose Steen found everything about him fascinating? Or mayhap because she'd lain in his arms the entire night. Made love to him more times than he could remember.

Och, nay, I remember. I remember every kiss, every caress, every way I took her. I remember the feel of her, the taste of her. She is honey, most rare and precious. Delicate like that of the bumblebee. Everything about the lass is etched into my soul.

He kept her close by his side as he guided her back down the pathway to her cottage. The sun might be up, but the path was still slick. The rain had turned to snow sometime during the night and snow and ice lingered in the shadows. He'd not have the lass injured in any way.

*Emma Rose is a part of me now. I hae been graced wi' both magic and a miracle. She can ne'er leave Scotia. She is mine. She belongs wi' me.*

*But how would he keep her? Was it merely a matter of convincing her to stay? What about these Colonies of hers, this city of the Phoenix? Were there rules about where one could and couldn't live?*

*John knew next to nothing of modern societies. It occurred to him that it might be difficult for her to make a permanent move to Scotland.*

*The lass will hae to gi' up her life in this Phoenix of hers. Mayhap she does'nae wish to do so. Mayhap she is in love wi' another man.*

*He recalled something she'd said about a marriage. Or had he dreamed that?*

*"Emma."*

*"Yes?" She looked up at him, expectant.*

*He hesitated. He did not wish to pry, but he needed to clarify the matter. "Are ye spoken for? Are ye wed?"*

*Her mouth dropped open and she stopped in her tracks. "Are you asking me if I'm engaged or married?"*

*"Aye."*

*"I guess you weren't listening last night. Or, maybe we were busy with other things." She shot him a crooked grin. "No, I'm not married. If I were married, or even engaged, I would not have done that. You know, what we did all night long." She pointed back the way they'd come. "It's not right to do that with one man when*

*you are married to another."*

*"Good." He took her arm and propelled her forward.*

*"I was married. Once. I mean, if you were wondering why I'm not a virgin and all that." She stopped again. "I should probably shut up now."*

*"I must apologize, lass. Are ye a widow, then?"*

*A corner of her mouth turned up. She tilted her head. "In a manner of speaking I guess I am, or I was a widow. He was sort of dead, but not like you." Her face turned red. "Sorry. I don't mean to make light of the subject, either subject. I don't know how you Scots feel about divorce, or felt about it back when you were alive, but I'm divorced. Divorce is pretty common with us. It was a bad decision to marry in the first place. I thought I loved him, well, I convinced myself I loved him. I'm rambling again, aren't I? I seem to do that a lot when I'm with you." Emma felt an additional explanation was in order. "But I'm guessing I married him so fast because of what my great-grandmother..." Her eyes opened wide and she stepped back a few paces, looking him up and down. "Holy crap."*

*John couldn't help but laugh at her exclamation. "I din'nae know what holy crap is but it does no' sound verra appetizing."*

*"No. Appetizing it is not. It's an expression of surprise. It means, wow, or oh, my gosh, or, well, in French it would be merde. I assume you speak French?"*

*John nodded. "Not for some time now, but aye. What is this merde?"*

*"Long ago, well, I don't know, thirteen, fourteen years ago, my great-grandmother*

*told me I would never love any man alive."*

*John stared at her. He wasn't sure if he'd heard her correctly. Never love any man alive?*

*Emma seemed to struggle to find the right words. "Do you know what a Gypsy is, or a fortune teller?"*

*"Aye, I hae heard of them."*

*"She read my tea leaves. It's a thing she does or did. She's since passed on."*

*"I am sorry to hear that."*

*"Thank you. But that's not the point. The point is when she read my tea leaves, she said I would never be satisfied by any man alive. She couldn't explain it and I didn't know what she meant, or what the tea leaves meant until this very moment."*

*Emma stepped in front of him. "John, you're not alive. Do you understand what I'm saying?"*

*John stood stock still. Hearing her voice echo his own thoughts was almost too much to contemplate.*

*"You are not a living man. But you are the man of my dreams. You are the man I want." She placed a hand on his arm. "I know it makes no sense. We don't know each other, not really, but what I want is a man like you. A good man. A real man, honest, forthright, true. My ex-husband was not true to me. He was not an honest man in either our marriage bed or our business arrangements.*

*"I just met you, John Charles McGregor, but I trust you and I feel like I've, oh,*

ow do I put this? I feel like I've known you, in here," she placed a hand over her eart, "my entire life. You are the man I've looked for, hoped for, prayed for. And ow I need to sit down before I fall down in a dead faint."

John scooped her into his arms. He looked around for a rock for the two of them. He didn't want Emma sitting on the cold, wet ground. He finally settled for using his ap as her chair while he sat on the cold, wet ground.

He rested his chin on the top of her head. "Emma Rose, ye are woman enough to make a man rise from the dead."

He heard her laugh. The soft sound warmed him through and through.

"Aye, ye are most verra powerful, with yer funny speech and yer modern ways." He glanced down the trail and across the loch where the morning sun illuminated the red stones of Urquhardt Castle. "T'was a beautiful sight a'fore the English blew it down."

"The castle?"

"Aye."

"John?"

"Aye?"

"Make love to me again, right here, in sight of the castle."

"On the pathway?"

"Aye," she said.

"Nay. There." He pointed toward the trees. "Some heather lingers beyond the pines. I will love ye in the heather if yer willing."

Emma leaned her head back to look up at him. "Oh yes. A thousand times, yes. In the heather on the hill, just like in Brigadoon."

"I hae ne'er heard of Brigadoon, lass, but if there is heather it must be a verra pleasant place."

Emma stilled for a moment and she shifted her gaze to the far-off castle. She said, "This is Brigadoon, John. I realize that now. You and I are in Brigadoon. Promise me you won't fall asleep. Not yet."

He caressed the glory of her unbound hair. Felt her shiver beneath his fingers.

"Ye are a strange one, Emma Rose. I will'nae sleep unless ye are in my arms. I promise."

Emma sighed then, a portentous sigh, and John wondered if he'd said the wrong thing or if there was something unsettling about this place called Brigadoon. But no, she smiled a smile brimming with promise and rose to her feet. She extended her hand to him and led him to the heather on the hill.

\* \* \*

"Emma Rose, I must leave ye."

"Hmmmm?" Emma still dozed, enveloped in the warmth of his hunting plaid and the fragrance of the heather.

"I must leave ye, Emma Rose. 'Tis no' what I had planned, but it seems I hae no choice in the matter."

*Emma sat bolt upright. "What?"*

*Her brain wasn't yet fully charged, not after so much loving and so little sleep, but she was conscious of a change in tone, in both the tone and tenor of John's voice. And it scared her to death.*

*Then the awareness of what he'd said sunk in and just like that she was wide awake. If John said he was leaving it meant he was leaving, as in leaving this world, her world. The word didn't mean he was going behind the rocks for a moment of privacy.*

*She reached for him, reached for him where he knelt beside her in the heather. But her hand slid right through his arm. There was no there, there. No arm to grasp. An image of John knelt there, nothing more substantial than that.*

*"No." Emma shook her head, fought her rising panic. "You can't leave, not after this. Not after what's happened between us. You promised."*

*He repeated, "'Tis no' my choice." He smiled at her, reached out a hand to caress her cheek, a hand she couldn't feel. "'But I must leave ye. It is the way of things. If it were up to me I would'nae leave ye, Emma Rose. I would stay wi' ye for the rest of yer life and I would meet ye in death."*

*"Don't go."*

*Emma looked around, hoping to see an angel, a demon, someone, anyone with whom she could argue. She wanted to protest his passing. It wasn't fair. None of this was fair. John had waited centuries for some resolution. But to resolve it now? And in this way? To rip him from her arms?*

*"You can't go, John. You can't. I want you to stay." Emma was up on her knees now, his plaid clutched to her throat. "I want you to stay with me."*

*He shook his head, the same gentle smile on his lips. "Ye will be fine, Emma Rose. I know it in here." He placed a hand over his heart. "Leatsa gu sìorraidh, nad chridhe gu bràth."*

*He was fading right before her eyes.*

*"What? What does that mean? John, what does that mean?"*

*"Ye hae set me free, Emma Rose. It means, I'll forever be with you, always in your heart."*

*And he vanished from sight.*

*Emma's mouth hung open and she could hear her own rapid breathing, but she was too stunned to make a single sound, to say a word.*

*If she was screaming, well, her screams were silent.*

*This can't be happening. He can't... This can't...*

*She sat back down in the heather, more alone than she'd been in her entire life.*

*He was so real. He was the most real person I've ever known. How can this be? How can this happen? What do I do now? What am I supposed to do?*

*Emma felt like she was about to have a panic attack. She couldn't manage to slow the beating of her heart. The past forty-eight hours had been surreal. The present moment was surreal too. It was all surreal. It was worse than surreal. It was flat out real unreal surreal, like so unreal it was real. Like she'd crossed some invisible boundary line where the unreal became real and the real, unreal.*

*I mean, am I even in Scotland? Am I dreaming? Have I imagined this entire trip?*

*Emma stood up and turned in a circle, desperate to latch onto something tangible, hoping maybe she could ground herself in the pines, the heather, the blue sky, the warmth of the sun, the bird calls.*

*But there was nothing to hold on to, no way to orient herself to this new reality. This reality empty of a man who had never been there in the first place, John Charles McGregor.*

*Wait. She looked down at her hands still gripping the plaid. I have this. I have his hunting plaid. Emma pulled it up to her face and inhaled. Yes. It still smelled like him, like smoke and man, a specific man, a man named John Charles McGregor.*

*Something flashed in the noon sun.*

*And what's that?*

*What on earth…?*

*Her eyes lit on an object half buried in the heather, something that reflected the bright midday light.*

*Did he leave something more?*

*Emma was forced to lift the hem of the plaid, so she could pick her way through the thick undergrowth.*

*She stood above his sword, his broadsword, the one with the McGregor crest. Emma was stunned.*

*What does it say? What did John tell me it says?*

*Emma forced her brain to focus, forced herself to remember his exact words.*

*That crest, it says... She closed her eyes to better concentrate on the memory of his voice.*

*"'S rioghal mo dhream, my race is royal."*

*Beside the broadsword lay his knife, his dirk.*

*Suddenly it was all too much. To possess a man for one night, to be possessed by him, yet lose him to death the next morning.*

*Emma dropped down into the heather.*

*What am I supposed to do now? How will I love any man alive after a night like this, a night spent in John's arms? Who would play such a cruel joke on both of us?*

*Why?*

*It was then that Emma knew with absolute certainty, without a single doubt, to the very depths of her soul, she had indeed spent the past twenty-four hours in the arms of a dead man.*

*She'd supped with a Highland ghost.*

*Emma buried her face in his plaid and sobbed.*

\* \* \*

*It was a long time before Emma ventured down to the shore of Loch Ness. A long time, as in three solid weeks. She'd spent as much time as possible in Inverness, away from the cottage.*

*At last she screwed up her courage, forced her feet to move down the path. She made a beeline for the place she'd encountered John, the rock where she'd first seen him, pebbles in hand. At the sight of the empty space Emma was tempted to turn back, but instead she squared her shoulders and forced her legs to keep walking. At last she reached the rock. She sat down, scooping up a handful of pebbles as she did so.*

*Emma stared out over the loch, wishing with all her might she'd hear John's voice. But she didn't hear his voice and she knew she never would.*

*I'm going to skip these pebbles. I'm going to skip them and then, when I've skipped enough pebbles, I'll figure out a way to find him.*

*At least I'll find what's left of his family.*

*As she picked through the rocks, searching for the right sized pebbles to skip, she couldn't help but see him in her mind's eye. She pictured him as he'd looked that day, as he'd looked the very first time she'd seen him.*

*He looked like a Norse god, no, a lonely Highland faery prince come down to earth to spend time with the little folk. To spend time with her.*

*Tears streaked her cheeks, but she ignored them and rose, holding the stones loose in her open palm. She would skip rocks in memory of John Charles McGregor, and by god, she'd skip them well because he deserved no less.*

*While she was skipping she'd let her mind work on the problem.*

*For there was a problem.*

*Her period was a week late. Emma was never ever late. Except when she was pregnant.*

*But she set that concern aside.*

*For now, she'd concentrate on the pebbles, or maybe not concentrate.*

*She'd let the stones go, let them do the work. Send them skimming over the glassy surface and with them, her sorrow.*

*Emma had been so selfish, so self-absorbed. She could kick herself in the butt. It wasn't about her. It had never been about her. It was about John. He'd left his purgatory behind, moved on. Somehow, she'd been the means, but the whys and hows and wherefores were beyond her comprehension.*

*I should be grateful. He's no longer stuck here, alone, haunting these mountains.*

*I am grateful. And humbled.*

*And determined to hold onto him, to hold onto his child. To keep his child safe.*

*I can do it. I will not lose this baby. If the gods or god or whoever took John away didn't have faith in me, they wouldn't have allowed this miracle.*

*She gazed out over the loch. Nothing stirred. The water was a mirror, reflecting the high clouds and the pink-gold light of the setting sun.*

*All right get to it, girl. Skip these dang stones.*

*The first stone plopped into the water with a splash. Emma snorted. It had been a long time since she'd tried skipping stones.*

*It didn't matter. The next attempt would be better. She knew it. And it was, a little.*

*"One. Two. All right. I can do this."*

*It took twenty minutes and a myriad of flat skipping stones to make it to a count of five skips.*

*"John skipped his pebble six times, so six it is, even if I have to stand here all night." Emma looked up. It wasn't yet full dark. Deep orange mingled with an even deeper crimson in the western sky.*

*If John was here, he'd call it the gloaming. Yes, if he was here.*

*Emma watched the crescent moon edge up over the eastern horizon. She caught its reflection in the ripples on the loch. Big ripples.*

*She looked down at the stones in her hand.*

*I didn't make those ripples. A second ago the lake, um, loch, was as still as glass.*

*And then she saw it, a big sleek wet dark head slip through the water twenty feet from shore. The body was so enormous and so black she could barely make it out in the dark water, but she could see its wake. The creature was big enough to leave a wake as it passed. She stared in astonishment.*

*Emma couldn't help herself. She was drawn to the creature like iron filings to a magnet.*

*She stepped into the shallows, shoes and all, and she kept going until she could no longer touch the bottom. She let the creature's expanding wake could wash over her. Wash her clean. Baptize her in the magic that was Scotland and Loch Ness, a three-*

*hundred-year-old ghost lover named John Charles McGregor and a miracle baby.*

*After all that, what could I possibly have to fear?*

*Emma heard John's voice, clear as day. "She eats fish. She does'nae eat people."*

*Emma treaded water, staring after her. At last the creature vanished into the depths and the ripples faded away. Emma swam back to shore. It was full dark now. She sloshed her way through the shallows.*

*She turned back to the loch and smiled, ignoring her wet clothes, squeaky shoes, and the chill wind.*

*She spoke to the monster. "I have nothing to fear. Nothing at all."*

*Emma knew what she would do with the rest of her life.*

\* \* \*

*Emma headed into Inverness. She wanted to stop by the rental agency, see if she could arrange to rent the cottage for an additional month. If she managed to achieve that task, she'd change her return ticket back to the States and keep the rental car. She needed the extra month.*

*John needed her.*

*There were some things only she could do for him, and for herself, to secure her future and to finish what he'd started. And he'd started something unimaginable.*

*He'd been left behind for a reason. She was his reason and therefore, he was hers. It was up to her to see that he received a decent burial, that his descendants knew the truth about what had happened to him.*

*Yeah, like they'll believe me.*

*Who knows? Maybe they will. So far Scotland hasn't exactly proven to be, well, ordinary.*

*When they see his body, the message he left for them, they'll believe me.*

*Concentrate.*

*Even though she had grown accustomed to driving on the wrong side of the road, or rather, the left side of the road, Emma reminded herself to focus. It wouldn't do to endanger herself or anyone else.*

*She found the rental office with ease. Over the past few weeks she'd discovered Inverness to be user-friendly. Everything she needed was within walking distance, once she'd found a parking spot. She'd hiked from one end of town to the other many times in recent days. Sometimes in shock and despair. Sometimes in contemplation. Most times in utter silence.*

*But all the while her hopes were stirring. Apparently, her brain was deep into stealth meal planning and recipes despite her determination to mope.*

*Emma's brain wanted to do stuff. It had lived the life of a pot set on simmer long enough. John Charles McGregor had increased the heat to high and her brain demanded that she attend. The encounter with Nessie had clinched it. Emma realized that, like the book said, she couldn't go home again. At least she couldn't go home the same person. She had changed in the past month. Everything had changed.*

*Time to get cooking, lass.*

\* \* \*

"Hello."

The woman behind the information desk lifted her head. She smiled in a friendly way. "Hello, miss. How may I help you?"

Emma hesitated. What if I get in big trouble? What if I'm accused of stealing relics or something? "This is a weird question, but do you have a McGregor here?"

The woman laughed. She gestured toward the wide modern glass door. "We have many McGregors here, although they would have been mixed among the other clans. They might be Stewart, or MacAlpin, MacNish, Menzies. I'm sorry, there's not a specific McGregor clan stone. The McGregors took many names after their clan was officially outlawed." She reached for a pamphlet. "You can follow the map and find all the clan stones."

"No, I know," said Emma. "I've spent hours walking the entire battlefield." She had. And the sight of the small battlefield, the clan stones, had rocked her. She could picture the blood and gore, sense the fear, feel the horror, the death. She swore she could smell the acrid tang of gun powder. She'd paid special attention to the boggy area, the area where the worst of the fighting had occurred, where John had told her he'd fought his way through the English line, where he'd climbed up a rise and caught that brief glimpse of the prince fleeing the field.

"I'm not asking about a McGregor clan stone," she said. "I know Clan Gregor, or the McGregors, took other clan names. What I mean is, do you have a McGregor here with whom I can speak? I have a few questions about the McGregors who participated in the battle and the librarian in Inverness told me I might find a McGregor here." Emma shrugged. "I'm a little reluctant to drive down to Perthshire. Although I guess I could find a McGregor or two down there."

"Aye, that ye could," the woman said, sounding like a Scot at last.

Emma thought the woman might laugh at her, but instead she nodded her head. "There is a docent here, a brilliant man. He's an historian and a natural born storyteller. His name is Malcolm McGregor. He's related to the clan chieftain, but then I suppose most McGregors are related to the chieftain. He's giving a tour right now." She glanced at her watch. "He should be finished in about thirty minutes. Would ye care to wait?"

"Yes, thank you." Emma looked around for a place to sit.

"Yer welcome to sit in the office if ye wish." She tilted her head toward an open door right behind the desk. "I keep hot water in there. Help yerself to a cup o' tea."

"You're very kind."

"Well, ye do look a bit peaked. How far along are ye?"

Emma's mouth dropped open. "How...? How did you know?"

"I've had three bairns myself. I know the signs."

"I'm just a, um, five weeks or so."

"I think ye should sit down a'fore ye fall down." The woman patted her hand. "I can assure ye it will pass. In another few months ye'll be feeling fine, better than e'er.

*Now go, sit, lass. Hae' yerself a cup o' tea."*

*Emma made a cup of tea and sat down to wait. Up until now no one else had known she was pregnant. It had been a big secret, shared by herself and the pee stick. But she was okay with this. The woman reminded her of a combination of her mother and John. It was the concern mixed with the brogue. Words have way more import when uttered in a Scottish brogue.*

*She sipped her tea, hoping it would calm her churning stomach. It wasn't so much the pregnancy causing nausea as it was the anxiety she felt about telling her story. The man was bound to think she was crazy as a loon.*

*But once he sees the broadsword and the dirk? At least he'll believe a portion of my tale and he'll make sure the authorities come to gather John's remains.*

*I wonder if John would prefer to be buried on Skye near his wife. Perhaps he'd rather be laid to rest on the traditional Clan McGregor lands. Well, it's not up to me.*

*They lived, John Charles McGregor. I wish I could tell you. Your wife took the baby and she fled Raasay, sheltered with the MacLeods of Dunvegan.*

*You didn't fail them, John. They survived.*

*Emma couldn't resist a smile.*

*You have many descendants. Some are famous. Some even went to Iowa.*

*How do you like those apples, John? Some of your descendants headed west, as we say, to found McGregor, Iowa. It's a small town on the Mississippi River, a big river.*

*I've seen pictures of the place. I bet you'd like it. It's quaint, beautiful. Wooded.*

*Granite cliffs. Deep valleys. Reminds me of the Highlands. Perhaps that's why the area appealed to your great-great-grandson, John Charles McGregor. He was one of the first men to follow his cousin, the founder of the community, Alexander McGregor.*

*It's listed on the Register of Historic Places.*

*I plan to stop there when I get back to the States. I want to see it for myself.*

*And then I'm selling my house and coming back to Scotland. You see, you're here so I have no choice. I want to be near you.*

*She heard John's voice. "Oh, ye always have a choice, lassie. The trick is to make the right choice."*

*"Miss?"*

*Emma's head flew up. For a moment she expected to see John. She'd been dreaming, or something like it. Maybe daydreaming, maybe dozing.*

*A man stood there, in full Scottish regalia—kilt, dark blue jacket, knee-high socks, dirk, sporran. He was the complete package. His gray hair made him look calm, distinguished, wise. He looked like someone who possessed all the answers to her questions. Or maybe not. Maybe all she needed was a person who would not run screaming for the mountains when he heard her tall tale.*

*He smiled.*

*Emma rose from her chair. "How do you do? I'm Emma Rose Steen, from America."*

*He took her hand. He had a firm grip.*

*"Steen you say? Steen with an ee or Stein with an ei?"*

*"Ee."*

*"Ah, a good Scottish lass. I'm Dr. McGregor. How may I help you?"*

*And just like that, Emma was at a loss for words. She knew her mouth was open, but nothing came out.*

*Dr. McGregor seemed to sense her discomfort. "Would you care to walk a bit? I often find it's easier to walk and talk, seems less formal."*

*Emma nodded. "Sounds like a good idea."*

*Now, where to begin?*

\* \* \*

*"I'm pregnant." Emma blurted it out. She stopped stone still in the middle of the path. She glanced over at Dr. McGregor. "Well, I guess I don't get a do over, do I?"*

*The professor let out a snort of laughter. "This is what I love about you Yanks. Not in your nature to dissemble. In the brain, out the mouth, I always say."*

*Emma smiled at him. "Yeah, well, hold onto your hat, it gets worse. I'm about to blurt out a whole bunch of brain stuff." Emma took a deep breath. "The father of my baby is a three-hundred-year-old Highlander by the name of John Charles McGregor. He was from Raasay and he fought with some other McGregors, including his brothers, his cousins, his uncles, his friends. They fought under John Drummond, Master of Strathallan. I think it was the Duke of Perth's regiment. He fought his way through Cumberland's line, right over there." Emma pointed to the boggy field. "He* called him The Butcher Cumberland.''

"Aye, that's how he was known, The Butcher."

Seems like everyone reverts to the vernacular in conversation with me.

"John managed to make it to the mountains above Loch Ness, near the Falls of Foyers. I'm renting a self-catering cottage on the shore of the loch. That's where we met. But that's not important. What is important is that John took shelter in a cave. He's still there."

"Still there mucking about the falls, is he?"

"No. He's gone now."

"Gone where?"

Emma's eyes filled with tears. "Just gone. Dead and gone. His remains are there. And a message. He left a message. He carved it into the rock wall of the cave, probably with his knife, his dirk." She put a hand over her belly. "I'm barely pregnant. I've lost two babies already. I don't plan to lose this child."

Dr. McGregor seemed sympathetic, at least to all appearances. He mumbled something that sounded like, "There. There." He took her arm. "Let's continue on, shall we?"

Emma followed his lead. "You don't believe me."

"I have no evidence as to his existence so I can'nae say I either believe or disbelieve ye."

"His wife's name was Tessa MacLeod McGregor. I've been to Skye, seen her *grave. When John didn't return, she sought sanctuary on Skye with the MacLeods of Dunvegan. She had relatives there, so she was welcomed. I guess the MacLeod's of Dunvegan and Raasay didn't exactly see eye to eye about the bonny prince."*

*The professor nodded. "'Tis true."*

*"She and John had a son, James Alexander McGregor. I believe he made his way to the Colonies. And I'm pretty sure his great-grandson ended up following Alexander McGregor to Iowa."*

*This time the professor stopped. "McGregor, Iowa?"*

*Emma nodded. "I understand Alexander McGregor, the man who established the town, was a descendant of Rob Roy. I've practiced, but I'm afraid you'll have to forgive my pronunciation. I'm trying to say this exactly the way John said it. 'S rioghal mo dhream. My race is royal. John told me that is the McGregor motto. It's on the crest. He showed it to me."*

*Dr. McGregor seemed to study her. "Showed it to ye? Showed ye the crest? On what? A computer?"*

*"No. Would you come with me, Dr. McGregor? You can see what he left behind, and after you look at his things, I'd like to take you to his cave, well, you or the authorities. Are you willing?"*

*"To go to this cave right now?"*

*Emma snorted. "No, right now we just have to walk as far as my car."*

*"Do ye plan to kidnap me, then?"*

She looked him up and down. "It's a tiny car. You'd be a tight fit."

He smiled at her pathetic attempt at a joke.

"Will you come?"

"Aye, I'll humor ye, lass. Ye are a verra pretty young lady. I can'nae say no to such a pretty little thing as yerself."

"And you are a charmer, just like John. Must be in the McGregor blood." Emma took his hand in hers. "It's the brogue, you know. Does something weird to my brain cells." She tugged him toward the parking lot. "His things are in the boot of my car." When Dr. McGregor hesitated, she said, "You don't have to worry. I won't shove you inside, cross my heart."

"All right," he said. "Show me these wee ghostie things of yours, lass."

"Not mine," she said. "John's."

\* \* \*

On one of her trips to Inverness, Emma had procured the largest, longest florist box money could buy. She'd wrapped the broadsword and the dirk in the worn plaid, placed everything carefully in the box, then covered all with tissue paper.

The plaid was fragile, worn and threadbare. It meant the world to her. Emma didn't want it torn or ruined.

John had warmed her with this plaid, made love to her on this plaid; wrapped the two of them in it while they'd shared her meager lunch.

No, I don't want it damaged in any way. I don't want it destroyed.

*She opened the trunk of her rental car, then she turned to Dr. McGregor. "Please be careful. John's hunting plaid is almost three hundred years old."*

*He looked down at the florist box. "Ah, lass, ye brought an old man flowers."*

*"My dear Professor, what I've brought you is a million times better than a bouquet of flowers."*

\* \* \*

*Emma had made sure to keep a GPS record of the location of John's cave. She knew exactly where she was going, in fact, she'd memorized John's deliberately circuitous route. She guided the procession along the mountain pathways just as John had oh-so-recently guided her, although this day the weather was much better. The sun shone on the purple heather. The sight of the flowers hurt her heart as it did every time she passed through them, but she pressed on.*

*The group included Dr. McGregor, several forensic archaeologists, two anthropologists, a police inspector, another historian from the nearby university, and what seemed like an entire class of history students.*

*"So, you say there are remains?"*

*Emma glanced back. It was the police inspector. She shrugged. "Yes and no. He's been there for two hundred and seventy years. I know there aren't many scavengers in Scotland, not like we have in the States, but it seems…" Words failed her. John had died alone.*

*No, he didn't, Emma. You saw him. You were with him when he died, when he* really truly died. He didn't die alone.

She repositioned her backpack and moved faster, trying to put some distance between herself and the inspector. Dr. McGregor caught up to her. He was the only member of the expedition who knew the truth of the matter.

"Din'nae fash yerself, Emma Rose. He means well. He's merely doing his job."

"I know. Doesn't make it any easier for me." She smiled at the older man. "Sometimes you sound like John. It's a little weird."

"Weird good?"

"Aye, Dr. McGregor. Weird good. I hope the inspector doesn't hold me responsible. I'd hate to go to jail."

"Will'nae happen. This is why I brought the forensic archaeologists. They'll be able to date the find."

"And the writing? John's writing on the wall of the cave?"

"Aye, that too. I've brought the dirk, so they can perhaps get a match, perhaps some dust or scrapings. 'Tis a matter of great importance with us. We Scots take our history seriously, especially the courageous twisted saga of the McGregors."

"I know. John said to me, 'There is a need to test one's mettle. A desire to right old wrongs, especially for Clan Gregor.'"

"He spoke true."

Emma nodded. "I guess the McGregors had a lot of wrongs to right. But John didn't want to go. He didn't. He told me not everyone was thrilled to see the prince.

*He was one of those who had reservations, but he was a Scot. And so he fought. And so he died a useless death."*

*"He may hae died anyway. He was a McGregor."*

*"He said the same thing. But his son lived."*

*"Aye." Dr. McGregor switched back to plain old English. "What will you do, Emma Rose? When you return to the States, I mean."*

*She took a deep breath. "Sell my house. Move back here. I've been studying up on how to become a resident of Scotland." She caught the doubtful look on Dr. McGregor's face. She said, "I don't want to be far from John."*

*Dr. McGregor put a hand on her shoulder. "My dear lass, John Charles McGregor is no longer here. If you're telling me the truth, that he's been dead and gone for three hundred years, and, God help me, I believe you are, then I have this piece of advice for you. Do not tie your future to a dead man. Or your child's future. He wouldn't want that."*

*Emma bit her lip so hard she tasted blood. She licked at it, resenting the metallic taste. No, better blood than tears. She looked up the slope, trying to avoid Dr. McGregor's discerning eyes. The man missed nothing. "Before John disappeared, he said, 'Leatsa gu sìorraidh, nad chridhe gu bràth.' I think it means..."*

*"Forever with you, always in your heart." The professor finished the sentence for her. There you have it," he said. "He's with you wherever you go."*

\* \* \*

*Yeah, well that is the million-dollar question. Where do I want to go?* She'd asked herself this for weeks, since Dr. McGregor had pointed out the obvious.

Emma stared out the window, watched the icebergs floating far below. She'd traded in her first-class ticket for the cash. *I can always use cash.* It had cost her a bundle to rent the cottage and the car for an additional six weeks. She sat in coach this time, in the very back of the plane, all alone in the last row, a row with two seats.

Emma was grateful for the solitude. She didn't want to chat with a stranger. She wanted to be alone with her thoughts.

She'd had to stay that extra six weeks. She'd had to see John's bones safely interred on Skye, beside those of his wife.

The flight attendant pushed her food cart next to Emma's seat. Dinner was a choice of sandwiches, turkey or roast beef, or a plate of cheese and crackers. Emma had no appetite.

"No, thank you. Just a ginger ale, please. And may I keep the can?"

"Of course."

Emma settled back and nursed her soda. She hadn't suffered much morning sickness. Her queasy stomach tended to happen later in the day.

*It's funny. Here I am, almost three months pregnant, and even though my two previous pregnancies didn't work out, I haven't seen a doctor yet. Why is that?*

*Could it be because I don't want a doctor to tell me there's something wrong with this baby? Or even worse, there is no baby?*

*I know there's a baby. I don't want to explain how it came about.*

*Then don't explain. I can tell everyone I did what I fantasized about doing. I had dinner with a Highlander, and I wound up in bed with him. Nobody has to know he was a dead Highlander.*

*Emma had changed her travel plans, again. Instead of flying to Newark and then on to Sky Harbor and home, she was on a direct flight from London to Chicago. She intended to rent a car and take a road trip to McGregor, Iowa. John's great-great-grandson, another John Charles McGregor, had lived there and died there and was buried there. She needed to see the place for herself, assure herself that his descendants had not only survived but thrived.*

*It looked like a pretty place. At least the photos she'd seen online were pretty.*

*Emma turned back to the window. The sun reflected bright off the ocean below. Flying toward morning. That's what they were doing. They'd left London in the evening, but they were flying backwards. Back in time. Not far enough. Not far enough to reach John.*

*It doesn't matter what Dr. McGregor says. I'm selling my house. I need a new place, new faces. A fresh start. Emma leaned back and closed her eyes. She folded both hands over her belly.*

*A new place, laddie or lassie, that's what we need. We'll find a new place to be a family.*

\* \* \*

*McGregor, Iowa, was so unexpected. Emma walked up and down the main street, faced the forested granite hills and she was awed.*

*Wow. John would love this small town.*

*The town was pretty and clean and quaint and old-fashioned and friendly and in a natural setting unlike any place Emma had ever seen. There was the Missouri River, there were the bluffs, the forests. She'd never pictured a state like Iowa with forests. Somehow, she'd thought Iowa was nothing but cornfields stretching from one end of the state to the other.*

*She stopped into the Chamber of Commerce to read about the town. Everything was old, as in nineteenth century old. But the buildings were well-preserved. Pretty didn't do the town justice; beautiful was more like it.*

*Emma learned that McGregor sat smack dab in the middle of what was known as The Driftless Area. It had to do with glaciers and rivers and canyons and bedrock. She felt like she needed a geologist to interpret the landscape for her, but since none was available, she did the best she could.*

*For a small town, there was an awful lot to see.*

*"Excuse me?"*

*The young woman behind the desk lifted her head. She gave Emma a smile. "How may I help you?"*

*"Can you tell me where the McGregors are buried? I mean, which cemetery?"*

*The woman gave a little laugh. "Well, if you mean the founder of McGregor, he's not here. His wife moved back to Wisconsin and took Alexander McGregor's body with her. But there are other McGregors buried here and there. Do you have an interest in genealogy?"*

*Emma shook her head. "I'm curious. I was just in Scotland and I met some McGregors. I heard about McGregor, Iowa, and I wanted to see the town. I decided to make a last-minute side trip. It's lovely here; this is one of the nicest small towns I've seen."*

*"Thank you. We take pride in our community. We've got quite a storied history."*

*"So I hear."*

*The woman handed Emma a walking map. "You can see the cemeteries here, here and here. You can pretty much walk to any of them. Maybe try Eastman or Pleasant Grove. Those are two of the oldest. Most of the earliest residents had private family plots so the oldest McGregors might not be in one of the cemeteries."*

*"Thanks. I will take a look."*

*The woman gave her another smile. "Hope you find the right McGregor."*

*Emma stared at her, open mouthed, rendered speechless. Bet I look like an idiot. At last she said, "Yes, me too." Oh boy, that one hit the mark. What I wouldn't give to find the right McGregor.*

*She left the building and headed up the main street. One of the cemeteries, Pleasant Grove, was high up on a hill overlooking the river. Emma decided to start there.*

*Pleasant Grove, nice name for a cemetery. I like it.*

She glanced down at the map as she walked. *As long as I'm here, I may as well check out some of the town's other historic landmarks.*

"Whoa!" Emma ducked in the nick of time as a big bag of something flew right by her head. She had to grab a street lamp. It was either that or end up on her backside.

Big hands held her shoulders and kept her upright. "I am so sorry, miss. I didn't see you. I was loading some cake into my pickup and…"

Emma looked up, straight into the most gorgeous, the most male, the most familiar emerald green eyes.

*What? The? Bluidy? Hell?*

He tried to keep her steady, give her time to get her feet beneath her.

"Are you okay? Did I hurt you?"

Emma could barely breathe. She stared at him for the longest time. At last she whispered, "John?"

At first, he appeared confused, then he studied her face. He seemed curious. "Do I know you?"

Emma wasn't sure how to answer him, so she answered both ways. "Yes and no."

He laughed. "How much yes and how much no?"

*I think I'm going to faint. Again.*

"Miss? Miss? You don't look so hot. You need to sit down, right now. Come over here."

Before Emma could say boo, he lifted her in his arms and set her down on something *other than the sidewalk. It felt like the gate of a pickup truck.*

*"Put your head between your knees." He placed a hand on her back and gently lowered her head. "Just like that. Take a few nice slow breaths. Hey, George." He kept one hand on her back. "Bring me a cold bottle of water, will you? Thanks."*

*"Seems like you're always saving me, John."*

*"Hmmm? Did you say something, miss?"*

*Emma shook her bowed head.*

*"Here." He pressed a cold wet plastic bottle into her hand. "Think you can sit up long enough to maybe sip some of this water?"*

*Get a grip, Emma. You dealt with a dead John Charles McGregor. You can deal with a live one.*

*She raised her head and took a few sips. "Thank you."*

*He kept a hand on her shoulder. Emma knew he was worried she'd decide to take another nose dive.*

*"I'm fine," she said. "It was just a shock to see you. I wasn't expecting to see you, ever again. You are John Charles McGregor, aren't you?"*

*He smiled.*

*Oh he has such a winning smile.*

*"That's my name," he said. "But I don't know yours. I'm sorry. I don't know how I could forget a beautiful face like yours, but I sure don't remember you."*

*She stuck out her free hand. "I'm Emma, Emma Rose Steen. We met a long time ago, a lifetime ago, I guess you could say."*

*His grip was warm. He made Emma tingle from the tips of her toes to the ends of her hair.*

*"A lifetime ago, you say?" John Charles McGregor grinned at her. "Seems like we're way overdue."*

*Emma tried to tamp down the hope in her heart. "Way overdue for what?"*

*"For getting reacquainted."*

\* \* \*

*"Mommy?"*

*Emma turned over, still half-asleep. She put an arm around her little daughter. "It's early, Tessie. Go back to bed."*

*"But mommy, daddy says he'll help me saddle up Dusty and I can move pairs."*

*Emma propped herself up on her elbows, her pregnant belly getting in the way. "Oh? I thought you were coming into town today to bake cookies with Jamie and me."*

*"Jamie's only three. He can't bake cookies. He just makes a mess."*

*"That's why I need you." She ruffled her five-year-old daughter's curly red hair.*

*"I'd rather ride my horse."*

*Emma grinned at her. "I'm teasing. I know you'd rather ride your horse. Tell daddy it's okay with me. But you have to wear your helmet."*

*"Nooooo, I don't want to wear my helmet."*

*"Helmet or no horse."*

*Her daughter let out a big exasperated sigh. "Okay I'll wear the stupid helmet. What kind of cookies are you gonna bake?"*

*"Your favorite, chocolate butter cookies with a salted caramel drizzle."*

*"Oooh!" Tessie clapped her hands with delight. "Bring me some."*

*"I will, but I have to leave most for the coffee shop. Speaking of which, I smell coffee."*

*"Daddy and Jamie are having breakfast. I already ate."*

*"Well, then I guess I'm a lazy bones."*

*Tessie climbed into bed with her for a cuddle. "But you have an excuse."*

*Emma nuzzled her daughter's neck. "Yes I do."*

*"Tessie." Emma and Tessie both looked up at the sound of a male voice. "Take your little brother and help him get dressed. Then you and I can saddle up."*

*Tessie hopped out of bed, eager to please and to get to her horse. She took her brother by the hand and after he got a kiss from his mother, she led him from the bedroom. "C'mon, Jamie."*

*John took Tessie's place in bed, took his wife in his arms. Held her close.*

*Emma not only loved with all her heart and soul, she felt loved, cherished.*

*"I had a dream last night."*

*"Oh?"*

*"It was a strange dream."*

*"What did you dream?"*

John said, "I was in a cave. I don't know where, in the mountains maybe. It was cold. I know that. And I was alone. I'd never felt so alone, at least I don't recall ever feeling so alone. Not in real life, anyway."

Emma felt a sudden chill. Of course she pictured John's cave above Loch Ness. How could she not? Her experience was something she and John had discussed, but not in great detail. He hadn't been comfortable discussing his ancestor's fate, no matter how real he'd been, no matter that he was Tessie's biological father. John considered himself Tessie's biological father, and truth be told, Emma knew deep down that he really was Tessie's father no matter how improbable it seemed.

"I had a knife. I used it to scratch something in the cave wall. It took me a long time to finish but I did it because I wanted someone to know I'd been there, when I'd been there."

Emma felt like she was listening to another story, one told by another John Charles McGregor, or a previous incarnation of the same John Charles McGregor. "What did you carve into the cave wall?"

It seemed like her husband hesitated. At last he said, "John Charles McGregor, born April 13 in the year of our Lord 1715. Died in the year of our Lord 1745."

The lump in Emma's throat was big enough to choke one of their horses. "I'm so sorry, John. I should have told you."

"That wasn't the end of the dream," he said. He rubbed a gentle hand over her belly.

*"What else? What else was there?"*

*"I wasn't in the cave. I was at the shore of a lake. It was a deep lake, a dark lake, in a valley. Mountains on both sides."*

*"What were you doing at the lake?"*

*"I was skipping stones."*

*Emma laughed despite the tears that filled her eyes. "Skipping stones. I believe that."*

*John laughed too, a little, but his voice sounded dead serious. "I was skipping stones, all alone. I had this feeling I was always alone. But out of the blue someone spoke to me. To me. Not to someone else, not to herself, but to me."*

*"What did she say?"*

*"Six. That's pretty good. I've never been able to skip a rock more than three times myself."*

*"Oh my god…"*

*"The first time you saw him that's what you said to him, wasn't it?"*

*"Yes." Emma held her breath.*

*"My name is John Charles McGregor. I was born and raised outside of McGregor, Iowa. I'm a rancher. I raise Angus beef like my father did and his father before him. I have two children, another on the way, and a wife I love more than life itself. I'm him, aren't I?"*

*"You're not asking me, you're telling me."*

"Yes." John stroked her hair. "I'm telling you."

"I believe so," she said. "I believe you and he are the same person. I don't know how. I don't know why. But I believe it to be true."

John rested his cheek against hers. He lay quiet, just holding her.

At last John said, "He's a lucky man. I'm a lucky man."

"Oh no," said Emma. "I'm the lucky one. I'm lucky you didn't bean me with that fifty-pound bag of cow cake."

John's laughter shook the entire bed. "Yes, woman, you are."

Emma heard the children clomping down the hallway in their cowboy boots. "We mustn't get too serious about these things, John. We've both been given a second chance even though you can't remember your first. That's all. I'm grateful. I'm happy. That's all we can ask." She sat up in bed, pulled him up with her. "Now, I have pastries to bake and you have cattle to move. And we have a life to live."

John leaned his head down for a kiss. His mouth close to hers, he whispered, "I said something to you in the dream. I don't know what it means."

"What did you say?"

"Leatsa gu sìorraidh, nad chridhe gu bràth."

Emma replied, "Forever with you, always in your heart."

And then he kissed her. Emma knew the truth. He had her with that kiss.

John Charles McGregor had always had her.

The End

*Thank you so much for buying this novella. If you enjoyed my Highlander, please check out my other work! J.R. Barrett*

Made in United States
Orlando, FL
03 July 2024

48561613R00071